RUIN
& other stories

EMMA HISLOP

TE HERENGA WAKA
UNIVERSITY PRESS

Te Herenga Waka University Press
PO Box 600, Wellington
New Zealand
teherengawakapress.co.nz

A catalogue record is available from the
National Library of New Zealand.

ISBN 978-1-77692-066-2

The writing and publication of this book
were generously supported by

Printed in Singapore by Markono Print Media Ltd Pte

For my family

Contents

Fur

The underground is hot and airless, and Nina wants to vomit. But that would be *the last straw*. Angela said *this is the last straw* when she came to get her from school and said it again on the walk to the station. Angela is her au pair. She'd had to cancel her hair appointment.

It's Ms O'Donaghue's fault. Her black skirt with white bobbly bits on it made Nina think of clouds and she wanted to feel it. Nobody saw her go underneath the desks. *Working independently.* She put her hand up Ms O'Donaghue's skirt to feel the material from the inside. *Inappropriate touching.* The rushing in Nina's head made it feel like her head was going to fly off her neck.

At Elephant and Castle lots of people get off and more people get on. Nina's tongue is dry, and her legs are itchy on the seat. The underground lights hurt her eyes. She leans forward and puts her elbows on her knees, balancing her weight. She can feel Angela watching her.

A man moves up the aisle and stands facing Nina, holding onto the yellow pole with one hand. The man's legs are covered in black fur – thick and soft, like a carpet or a rug. The fur grows around the man's knees, making two holes, like holes in an old jumper and his sandals look wrong at the end of his legs, like they've been stuck on. Bits of fur poke through the gaps and stick out like tangled grass. Fur hangs down out of the man's shirt sleeves, and covers his arms, stopping at his wrists. It stops suddenly in a neat line like Miss O'Donaghue draws with a ruler – Nina slides her fingers along her thighs towards the man. She watches her hand stretching out; she can almost put one finger on the man's wrist and stroke that straight line. *This is the last straw. Inappropriate touching.* She pulls both her hands in towards her body and folds her arms over her chest. The back of her neck is starting to sweat. Her shirt sticks to her back. Disgusting. She sits back in the seat and exhales. Everybody else has a pet. It isn't fair. A cat or a dog or any kind of pet with fur would do. Angela gave her a goldfish. Goldfish are boring.

At Borough station the person beside Nina gets off and the furry man sits down in the seat. Nina's head rushes. *Look away don't touch.* She can smell Angela's perfume. It's mixing in with people's sweat and it's everywhere. It's on her tongue. Her tongue feels thick and fat and her throat is filling up. She opens her mouth then closes it. She looks up at the advertisement on the ceiling. A lady in a headscarf. Underneath it says *I believe in women's rights and so did Muhammad.*

The man takes an iPhone out of his shirt pocket. Nina leans over and tries to look at the screen. Football results. The knuckles on the man's fingers sprout fur, single black wires curling up tightly at the ends. Nina looks at her own naked fingers. She tilts her head back and sideways, so her eyes are in line with the man's shoulder. The fur grows out of the man's collar and up his neck into the hair on his head. It is shiny and wet looking. The heat and airlessness are closing in. The man's legs are covered with silky strands all going in the same direction. He is so close that Nina could put her fingers there. *Remember to make good choices.* The man puts his iPhone away then leans his arm on the armrest. Nina straightens up in her seat and holds her head like a statue, eyes out in front. She blinks and brings her hand up beside the armrest. There is a moment of nothing while she steadies her hand. Slowly brushes the man's wrist with her finger. Strokes the straight line. The fur is velvety and smooth. The man shifts in his seat. Nina takes her hand away. Her head hurts and there is a buzzing noise in her ears. She closes her eyes, but it makes her feel dizzy. Better to keep her eyes open. Sit very still.

A trail of sweat runs down Nina's back. *You've nobody but yourself to blame.* She breathes in and she is putting her cheek on the man's arm, just resting it there like she's having a little sleep and closing her eyes. The fur pillow is on her cheek and for a moment everything is perfect. The wispy black threads are warm and a bit damp and Nina relaxes her weight, letting her face settle in. She breathes out. Pushes her fingers through the fur, burrowing into the thickness.

The man's arm jerks up, and Nina jerks upright in her seat. *Look at the person.* She screws her eyes up and holds tightly onto the armrest on the other side.

Angela's hands clasp Nina's waist pulling her up and *say sorry* and the underground sounds are tuning in and out like a radio. She buries her face in Angela's soft breasts and says *sorry sorry*.

Previous Selves

'You're spending a lot of time away from your place,' Faith says. 'I don't want you to feel like you have to spend every night with me.'

He frowns. 'It doesn't bother me.'

It's a surprise when Drew holds her hand across the table later that night and says he wants to come to New Zealand with her. His face seems kind in the dimly lit bar. Four or five times a week for the past six months they've met up for a drink, then spent the night. She's been thinking of going home for a while, sick of paying so much rent for her tiny London apartment. Though the apartment has been one of her most stable relationships over the last five years.

'I've always wanted to go,' he says. 'All those bush walks, that mountain that looks like Mt Fuji. And I can work anywhere.' He orders an expensive bottle of wine and talks some more, making a good case, including London being filthy and Boris Johnson. That moment feels a bit like a completed puzzle, and she surprises herself by agreeing. They'll try it for a year, two at the most. They drink the wine and it's like he's lit up.

They walk to her flat and stop in a doorway to kiss and touch. They go to bed. He usually likes to get deep inside her but tonight he's too gentle and he comes, and she doesn't. Afterwards he slips his hand in hers and talks about things he hasn't before, his family who she hasn't met, his father, who was a brain surgeon.

'We didn't get on,' he says. 'He'd asked me to go hiking with him and I said I was too busy. He'd been dead for days when a ranger found him.'

Faith pictures her own family tree, rolled out across the lounge floor at her parents' place. Her eyes are heavy.

'We'll be fine,' he says, and she doesn't know what he's talking about, and she falls asleep.

The New Zealand flat comes furnished and Faith gets a job as a photographer for the *Daily News*, with a staff car. New houses have been built along the seafront since her last visit, huge modern boxes made from wood and corrugated iron. The shadows on the sea have a stark, vivid quality. The mountain is covered in snow already and everything below the snow line is green and she can feel the sea air in her lungs.

On their first date, Drew talked about his job as an independent programmer. Because it was online, he explained, it was hard to meet people, and though he wanted people to know him, online he couldn't really be himself, so instead he gave Tinder a go. So far it had only made him feel more alone.

'Going out for dinner on your own – it's depressing,' he'd said, waving a hand. 'Really, I just eat a lot of takeaways.' Faith had been sitting on the couch beside him, and though he'd muted his phone, sometimes it vibrated, and he'd stop talking a moment, and Faith sat there looking at him – fuck he was handsome – waiting for the story to end. Months later, she thought how typical that was, him telling her about a problem that existed only in his head yet making her wait while he checked his messages. She'd later questioned a lot of things.

Back in Aotearoa, her parents and her old friends are a

reminder of who she used to be. In her friends she sees all their previous selves, just as they must see hers in her – teenage girls at the White Hart, confiscated hip flasks, crimped hair and house parties they weren't invited to.

The mountain flows with cold and he complains incessantly about the lack of central heating. They binge-watch true crime shows under the duvet and eat takeaways and fuck and sleep with their bodies pressed together. Faith leaves for work in the mornings when he is still curled up warmly in bed. She doesn't know what he does all day. When she asks him about work, he says it's not interesting, that she doesn't want to hear about that. She can't tell him she misses him when she's at work, although she does and at the same time wishes he'd go away.

It's hot in the living room when Faith gets home from work on Friday. She makes her way across the debris on the floor – computer magazines, barley sugar wrappers, a pizza box – to turn the heater off. She flicks it off at the wall and calls out but there's no answer. His laptop is on the sofa. She's not sure what prompts her to flip it open, but she does, and sees a conversation not meant for her. There are more girls, all slim and dark and pretty, like Faith at that age.

Renata and Jon invite them to a Matariki party. He'd rather stay home tonight, he says.

'They're good friends,' she says. 'You've hardly left the house.'

He drives with one hand on the wheel, the other resting on her thigh. It's not until they're almost there that Faith knows what it is. He's ruined everything. Did she even know the whole of it? The more she knew, the harder it was going to be to salvage things. Would she want to? She wants to push his hand off her leg, tell him to stop the car, let her out. He'd probably say she was making a scene. Instead, she almost crushes the container of pūriri seedlings she's balancing on her lap with a salad. They pull up to a row of parked cars in the drive. There's smoke from the bonfire and it's a full moon.

Renata opens the door. Behind her, the hallway is crowded with people and strung with coloured paper lanterns. The last time Faith saw some of these people they were teenagers and it's strange to see them now, in grown bodies.

'We were just saying how good looking he is.'

In the past, Faith's friends have accused her of being picky. She hands Renata the seedlings. They watch Drew shake hands with Jon. She thinks about all the years she'd lived in this place before he came here, all the time they'd been strangers to each other – were strangers.

'Babe,' Renata says, seeing Faith's face. 'What's wrong?'

Faith puts the salad on the table. She hasn't decided whether to tell Renata the girls were young. She has no way of knowing, not exactly. There's no way to get into it all here.

'I found something today on his computer,' she says to Renata. 'Now that I think about it, maybe I jumped to conclusions.'

'Don't tell me – he's into hardcore,' Renata says.

'They looked pretty young.'

'How young?'

It strikes Faith that her oldest friend is concerned. Renata who will say yes to most things because she can't say no. It's a good enough answer.

At the kitchen table, he sits with his legs crossed, reading the paper.

'I thought we might go for a drive,' he says. 'Stop and get another coffee somewhere.'

She stirs some milk into her porridge, can't bring herself to ask him. This isn't like him to suggest an outing, so she nods. What to say? A change of scene might help her figure it out. After breakfast they drive around. He leaves New Plymouth and heads south, towards the mountain. They pass the crematorium, then stretches of trees and farmland. They begin a slow, winding ascent. Trees bend over, forming a tunnel over the road, and they follow the road until the trees finally part. The Visitor Centre sits above the car park, where two other cars are pulled up.

He's paying at the tearoom counter and his driver's licence falls onto the floor. He looks moody in the photo, the same stubble, but taken a few years ago. But it's the date that gets her attention. When he turns, she hands it to him. His shoulders lift and fall like he's trying to relax but he doesn't say anything.

They sit in the window. The expanse of farmland is vast from up here, dwarfing the city. The coast sweeps around to Ngāmotu Beach and the port where the old power station chimney stands out. Paritutu rock, and the smaller islands around Back Beach. The silver sea is too bright to look at for long.

Faith coughs, clearing the dry feeling in her throat and says, 'I thought you said you were thirty-three.'

'Sorry?' He looks as if he hasn't heard right. 'What made you think that?'

'Your Tinder profile?'

He looks blank. Not playing.

'Come on, you put your age at thirty-three.'

'Faith, I haven't a clue what you're on about.'

'You could just tell me.' She's not sure why but the way she says it sounds like an apology. She stares across at him. She wants to take hold of him by the shoulders and shake him. Tell him he didn't need to lie to her, not to lie to her.

'You must have read it incorrectly. You do realise how crazy this sounds?' He smiles when he says it, but he's fed up with this, whatever it is.

'I just wondered why you lied.'

'You don't get to talk to people like this, Faith. It's childish.'

Faith closes her eyes. It's as though he thinks she's trying to trap him, make him tell something other than the facts.

'Christ, we've wasted the best part of the day. Can I assume the ridiculous questions are over now? Let's go for a walk.'

'I'm hardly dressed for it.' She's in a merino shift and slip-on shoes.

'There's some gear in the car. Although I'm not sure why everything is my responsibility.' Back at the car he pulls out new looking tramping boots in her size and thermals and jackets. She is at fault, somehow. He's standing behind her, holding out a jacket. He doesn't say anything, but Faith holds out her arms and he slips the jacket on. She lets him zip it up. 'About time you walked off some of those takeaways.'

Faith reaches hard inside herself, and finds it – finds a smile, and nods.

At first, it's beautiful. A bush track, clean air, the sound of tui and toutouwai. They pass another couple, coming back down and say hi. Twenty or thirty metres up, towards the top of the curve, is a smattering of snow, starkly contrasting against the deep green of the tree line. They walk in silence. She's trying to figure it out. She lies sometimes, without planning to, or knowing why. The boots are heavy. Her footprints leave dark marks on the track, fading to chalky white beneath them, worn into the snow. Ahead of them stretches a line of smoothly eroded footprints, set at regular intervals, and she walks in these until she is about halfway up, and the prints are lost in the snow. Maybe she'd read his age wrong, like he said. Faith looked younger than she was. Maybe the girls were old enough. He's further up the track and he turns and does that smile. The track is steeper here, and sloping. The trick is not to look down, and not to stop. Stopping makes things worse. She'd made that mistake once rock climbing on school camp, and her body had seized up. The words press at her mouth.

'Why didn't you introduce me to any of your friends?' she says.

'You met Owen, didn't you?'

'Only because we ran into him that day in Camden. What about your family?'

'Where are you going with this, Faith?'

'Nothing. Nowhere.' She says it too quickly. It occurs to her that she's scared of the lie, what it represents.

The wind gets up. The jacket feels too tight on her body. She takes her phone out of her bag and checks for a signal. It's low. Wind pushes her hair into her eyes, her mouth. She begins to descend the path and the slope propels her forward, so she half runs.

She goes into the gift shop at the front of the tearoom. The woman behind the counter is maybe sixteen, maybe younger. Her hair is scraped off her face and she isn't wearing any makeup. Faith can see the outline of her bra under her T-shirt. She tries to remember herself at that age. She'll just sit at this table for a moment and get her head together. He will tell her she's in the wrong, as she's been so many times before. The young woman is restocking the teas on display behind the counter.

'Excuse me.' It's him. He's in the gift shop. How did he

slip in here, unnoticed?

The woman stops what she's doing, turns and smiles. 'How can I help?'

'Well, that depends,' he says, looking at his watch. Faith wants to watch without thinking, but her thoughts spiral. He hasn't seen her. 'Quiet in here today.'

The woman smiles, nods. 'It is quiet.'

'Are you still doing coffee, by any chance?'

'I can do that for you,' she says.

'Good!' he says, as if approving of her. 'I thought you might be closing early.' He's looking, growing his smile and there's nothing else in the room and Faith wonders what she's given away.

Housewarming

It was three weeks after the miscarriage. Tae stood at the living-room window, watching guests arrive. It had seemed fine when Mike proposed it, months away, abstract. Right now, all she wanted to do was sit in bed with her laptop and a cup of tea. But they'd already postponed once. People were getting out of cars, gathering themselves, carrying plates of food. Most of the cars were unfamiliar, but her sister Nico's was among them. Sun hit the wedding cards on the mantelpiece. She thought about drinking. There was something she could do about that. There was a meeting that evening.

The living room was filling up with people she recognised from the wedding. She nodded and smiled at people who said hello, repeating their names in her head. There was friendly conversation – everyone wanted to see the renovations. People had brought their kids. There was no mention of a baby, or even a foetus. Christ, it was fifteen weeks. She needed to stop blaming herself for telling people. She straightened a picture on the wall in the hallway. Most of the artwork belonged to Mike. Some of Tae's clothes were still in boxes and her antique dressing table looked too big in their bedroom. She'd hoped that moving out here, with new people and surroundings, might let her be someone else too. Still, it was an adjustment.

As she walked down the hall towards the kitchen the front door opened and her nieces, four and five, ran down the hall, carrying papier-mâché shields. They'd sprayed them in gold paint and their hands were covered in it. They veered right into the new kitchen and out the back door into the garden.

The kitchen smelled of fresh paint and curry. Kath, the pastor, was standing at the island bench, taking cling film off a cake. The bench was covered in pies and cakes and jars of relish. Kath stopped and rested a hand on Tae's arm. She studied Tae's face and Tae wondered if Mike had said something to her about the miscarriage. But there would have been no reason for him to do that. They'd decided they'd only tell close friends.

'Are you sure you're up to this, love?'

Tae didn't want Kath's concern, but she nodded and smiled. Why had he told Kath? Who else had he told? It would have been easier not to say anything. Tae felt the tickle in her lungs. She swallowed once, twice. A cough. Kath looked even more concerned. Kath was a mother of three, or four, Tae wasn't sure of the exact number. Tae felt now would be a good time to get away, but Kath hadn't finished. She was filling a glass from the tap. Deep breaths wouldn't slow it, nor would drinking a glass of water.

'It's just allergies.' It wouldn't leave her alone. The doctor couldn't find anything else wrong. He'd asked a few questions. How was Tae feeling otherwise? Was she feeling depressed? Tae sipped the water and wondered what prayer she'd say if she was the kind of person who prayed. Wasn't prayer just confessing one's desire? It wasn't that Tae didn't know what she wanted, more that she had no control over the things that happened. Or that she desired impossible things. Like having a baby. And being able to have a couple of cold beers at the end of the day.

'Here you are,' Naomi said from behind her. Naomi

was Tae's close friend and flatmate from her last flat. She was coming up the steps, wearing a dress Tae hadn't seen before. Kath went to the door. Naomi held orange juice and champagne awkwardly in the crook of her arm as she shook Kath's hand. Then she was inside.

It was Naomi who had hooked Tae up with Mike, after Tae went to a psychic. Naomi was a lapsed Christian and she and Mike had been at Bible College together in their twenties. Tae felt stupid about it. She'd intended to get her financial shit together and pay off her student loan. But it was the psychic who predicted Tae would meet a Capricorn soulmate with a relationship to God.

'So, apparently, there's a Capricorn Christian boy waiting for me in the stars, Nomes.'

They were in the Paterson Street kitchen, after dinner. 'I went to see a psychic yesterday.' She couldn't tell the others, they'd judge her. She turned on the hot tap and waited. Although everyone had been nicer to her since she stopped drinking. Or was it that she was nicer? It was impossible to tell. Naomi was sitting at the kitchen table, looking at her computer.

'Nomes, are you even listening?' Tae measured the temperature with her fingers, then put the plug in the sink.

'Bible college Mike. Oh my god, yes, he's totally your type.'

'What's my type? Who's Mike?' She squeezed some dishwashing liquid into the water.

Naomi swung the laptop around on the table, displaying a Facebook profile.

'You're making this up.' Tae laughed, mostly because the idea was so ridiculous.

'I'm not making it up. And I just checked his star sign. It totally checks out.'

Tae had agreed to meet him. She could always blame Naomi when it didn't work out. They met for a coffee in town. Mike was tall, listening more than he spoke, more present than a lot of people. He was a youth worker. Afterwards they went to the art gallery and Tae tried to figure out if she liked him. He was definitely too young for her, with his smooth face and low-hanging jeans. It was a surprise to find out he was forty-two. After a month, Mike gave her a set of keys. Sometimes he'd crash in town at her flat on the weekends.

'You know, we could be saving money,' he said one morning. 'I could get rid of my flatmates, and you could live here. Save a fortune on petrol.' Mike had inherited some money from his grandmother in England. The house had been dark and cluttered with houseplants and the carpet smelled of mould. The renovations were Tae's idea – they'd ripped the carpet up then gutted the old kitchen. Next, they were replastering and repainting the bedrooms.

Tae's sister, Nico, came into the kitchen and gave Tae a hug. 'Traffic out here from town is a nightmare.' It wasn't even Wellington, not really, out this far.

'You're right on time,' Tae said.

'I'm pregnant,' Nico said, in Tae's ear. 'Fuck. Sorry.'

Tae's head was racing. 'What are you sorry for? How far along?' She balled up the tea towel in her hands, over and over. Her sister was due in May. Gregor wasn't thrilled but he'd go along with it.

'Are you feeling okay?' But Tae didn't hear what happened next, how Nico was feeling. Tae's second scan had shown an abnormality. They hadn't known then what it meant.

On the hob there were three pans, chattering and bouncing as they simmered and spilled their contents. People kept coming to the front door, forgetting about the renovation. Into the old entrance – now the open plan kitchen and dining room – and some people said 'sorry' and walked through but other people turned around and went to the back door. They should have put a sign up. One of the pans began to screech and Tae went over and turned it off.

Mike was still outside talking to the builder. Mike had been doing the rewiring, but he was in over his head. They were talking about the new gib. They were behind schedule but at least the kitchen was installed now, and Rob, the builder, wanted the weekend work.

'It's never the perfect time for a party, Tae,' Mike had said. 'Things are always going to crop up.'

'Things. Let's see, Mike: morning sickness, miscarriage, and a failed DIY job.' She'd insulted him, she saw that. But now there wasn't any cause for celebration.

When the first trimester had passed, Mike had called his family and close friends. Things seemed to be going well. They hadn't told many other people Tae was pregnant, although some must have guessed. But then, two weeks later he'd pulled out and there was blood. The midwife said there might be spotting, Tae had told him.

A jumble of plates and glasses crowded the large, rectangular dining table. Red candles down the middle picked up the pink and red of a serving dish. Tae was sure she'd heard one of the evangelical women from the church say 'a woman's touch'. Mike still hadn't gotten around to cleaning out the stuff left by previous tenants.

'I reckon I'll start the BBQ now,' Mike said in his easy way, coming in.

'Mike, can I borrow you for a minute?' Tae walked into

the laundry, and he followed her.

'You look great in those,' he said, pointing to her new jeans.

'Did you tell Kath? I felt like a fucking idiot just now.'

'She guessed, and I couldn't lie. People will find out eventually.'

Mike's own mother believed that the souls of the dead rose and became one with the universe. Mike didn't believe this anymore, but he often talked about God, as though they were best friends. Tae's only religious experiences had been drug-related, and she wore her atheism proudly. Tae had gone along to Mike's church a couple of times, hoping to hear something about how gay people should never marry or women who were date-raped shouldn't wear provocative clothing. Despite Kath's sermon going on too long, Tae hadn't heard anything that gave her any further proof that churches were corrupt.

'We had an agreement.'

'You'd rather Kath thought you were still pregnant? Wouldn't that be weird?'

'What's weird is everyone knowing intimate details of my life,' Tae said, her eyes filling up. 'I hardly know these people. Your people.' She couldn't turn off the part of her that wondered if everything was pointless.

'Oh, come on, that's ridiculous.' He laughed, but it was a defensive laugh, his face a mixture of hurt and care. 'And hardly – you've got your meetings.'

They went back into the kitchen. Kath was on her phone. He opened the fridge and handed Tae a Coke. Tae tried not to look at the bottles of wine lined up inside. She opened the Coke and imagined Mike holding their baby. Sometimes, when she closed her eyes, she could see their baby's face. Mike would have looked good as a dad; he could still look good.

She wanted to tell him, but she couldn't, not in front of Kath.

'That curry smells great. Oh hey, Ev.' Mike stepped outside.

Evie was wearing a yellow T-shirt with mountains printed across her chest and enormous sunglasses, which she didn't remove. She looked cute in everything. If she and Mike had been sitting, their knees might have touched. Evie was smiling at Tae and, when Tae looked at Mike, he was smiling at Evie.

'Oh, hey Evie.' Tae tried to sound positive. Evie, who had cried the first time Tae and Mike hooked up and hadn't been able to let it go.

Mike and Evie were dance partners in a rock-and-roll club. They were good. Around here, that made them a legend. People talked about them like they were one person, saying things like 'Man! How great was Evie and Mike?' Their routine was complicated, and they'd won some awards. Evie sewed their dance costumes and she reassured Mike when he doubted his abilities. They used Mike's living room for club meetings, and once when Tae was staying over, Tae lay in bed, listening to the sound of Evie's laugh, trying not to think about them together.

Evie was married, although Tae had only met her husband Ryan briefly, and she had guessed, or worked out from conversations with Naomi, that there had been sex outside of that relationship, though whether that was an affair, or a mutual arrangement, Tae didn't know. Evie was competition. Sometimes it felt like Mike and Evie had already fucked. No one was talking about it or acknowledging it. What if Evie did leave Ryan? Would Mike betray Tae that way? The thought made Tae crazy. She couldn't help asking the question: if Evie wasn't married, would Mike and Evie be together?

'It's a bit of a pointless question, though, isn't it, Tae? She is married,' Naomi reminded her, over coffee one day.

'What about if they broke up? Then what?'

'Tae. He's chosen to be with you.'

Sometimes, that answer was enough, and sometimes the question obsessed her. 'Maybe Mike's sending Evie mixed messages. Fuck, I don't know,' Tae said to Naomi. 'That would be unhelpful.'

'But what are those messages?' Naomi asked.

Tae didn't know, exactly – she was imagining Evie and Mike having sex. 'Like, I get that friendships can be complicated. But Mike doesn't share anything about his personal life with his clients. He says friendship creates an unhelpful bond.'

'Evie's not a client, Tae,' said Naomi.

'I bet it would be really athletic, fun sex.' Tae missed sex, missed the desire for sex. Before the miscarriage, she and Mike were having a lot of sex. Not drinking meant feeling things properly, and Tae spent a lot of time now thinking about what felt good. Everything turned her on. With Mike it was easy, he was so willing to give into her. When they had sex all she could think of was herself, how to get the most pleasure from it. All that seemed out of reach now.

'Maybe Mike led Evie on and made her feel special because it made him feel good; maybe it wasn't him not knowing what commitment was,' said Tae.

'Uh, he married you. Big commitment if you ask me,' said Naomi. She sighed. 'This is getting old, Tae.'

'Maybe he likes the attention,' said Tae.

The pregnancy changed things. She realised that she needed to put Evie away. She no longer wanted Evie there, in the present, making her heart circle around the past. Mike had offered to leave the club, but it didn't eat at Tae anymore. Even at the club fundraiser last month when the MC introduced Mike and Evie as the Hutt's hottest new couple. Tae tried to make eye contact with Evie, rubbing her belly in slow circles, but Evie hadn't looked in her direction. That didn't necessarily mean anything. She danced with confidence, changing the routine up, leaning into Mike more than was necessary, so their faces were almost touching. The body language was clear. Couldn't everyone else see it? When they finished, with a spinning lift that resembled a bride being carried over the threshold, Evie was out of breath, her face flushed. She was glowing. The applause came in waves. Tae went over and kissed Mike in front of everyone. Tae couldn't see Evie's face. Her fringe fell over her eyes.

Back at home, taking off her makeup in the bathroom, Tae watched a strand of her own hair float to the floor and blend into the Lino.

'You can't leave the club. You love the club.'

He agreed rock and roll made him happy.

The door opened, and shut after the fumbling of shoes being taken off. More of Tae's friends arrived, adding their coats and bags to the pile in the bedroom. Until recently, they had all lived together. Someone turned up the music in the living room. Mike stayed in the kitchen with four other people who had just arrived. Tae leaned against the door frame and watched as Mike showed them the new countertop, describing what a nightmare the sanding was, where the skylight was going in, when they could afford it.

'Which will be some time in 2050,' Tae said to Naomi and Shane. They had to figure out the budget.

'You've moved to the bloody sticks, T,' Shane said. Tae gave him a hug as he squeezed passed. 'Did you actually buy this house?'

'If one more person tells me it's a good investment, I'm

going to scream,' Tae said.

'You're living in a freaking flood zone. T, is there a shop around here? Where I can walk to buy cigarettes?'

'Back to the main road, then turn left. I thought you'd quit.'

'Oh shhh, please. I quit. Then I started again.' He walked out of the room. 'Back in a week unless I get lost.'

'How's everything at the flat?' Tae asked.

'We're being evicted,' Naomi said, making a face. 'Transit sent a letter last week, which listed the diseased walls, asbestos and the contaminated rat droppings.' The music was quieter again.

'Shit,' Tae said.

'Literally,' said Naomi.

'But you're staying on?' Tae didn't miss Shane that much, but Naomi was another story.

'Oh, I don't know. No. I'll move in with Pete for a bit.'

Naomi wanted to see the wedding photos. They sat on the bed and Tae swiped through them on her laptop. Her face had hurt from smiling by the end of the day. She remembered the feeling of being pregnant. That was what she remembered the most.

In the weeks before the wedding, Tae spent hours looking for a dress until she realised the problem wasn't the dress, but nothing fitted on her body like before. Naomi went to design school in the Nineties and knew a lot about fabrics. Silk and satin were too hard to work with and linen would crease.

'I really like that one,' Tae had said, pointing to a beautiful, patterned cotton.

'No logical progression in the seams,' Naomi vetoed. They were at the third store and Tae was hungry. She was beginning to think Naomi was winding her up.

'How do you feel?' Naomi asked, eventually.

'Fine,' she said.

'Morning sickness gone?'

'I feel fine. I'd be better if we could find some fabric.'

'How long is it now?'

'Three months, five days and counting.'

She had needed a blood transfusion, the doctors told her after the miscarriage. Mike was waiting when she was wheeled out of theatre, and he sat by the bed holding her hand until she fell asleep. The nurses had tried to kick him out at ten when visiting hours finished but he'd refused to go.

Tae swiped faster, concentrating on the screen. Chocolate icing from the cake had squished onto her dress and left a mark. She'd dabbed water on the worst bits. Tae wondered now how much of his proposal was shaped by his friends from church's questions when they found out she was pregnant. While she and Mike were seeing each other, it wasn't that serious yet. It was the elephant in the room, but he wasn't going to answer a question she hadn't asked.

Shane got back, reeking of cigarettes. 'What did you want to ask me about?'

'I have a situation,' Tae said, making sure Naomi wasn't in the vicinity. 'Two friends have become attracted to one another, even though they're both married.'

'I'm so here for this,' Shane said.

'After a while, one of them started seeing someone else, and now the other friend, the one who is married, is unhappy and feels the other person has led her on.'

'Have they?'

'Maybe, a bit. Really more of an emotional situation than any other situation,' Tae said.

'Without knowing more details, I'd say these things

usually work out, given time,' Shane patted her on the arm. 'Just sucks while you're in it, T.'

They set all the food on the table – various salads, a big tray of roast vegetables, the curries and the barbecue meat. Kath gave a blessing, but Tae couldn't hear. Everyone lined up and started assembling their food. People sat on the sofas and chairs, some on the floor. There was mud on the rug by the door. Tae ended up perched next to Evie on a bench at the end of the table. She felt Evie turn beside her, asking how her day was going. They were careful with each other. Tae swallowed her mouthful, complimented the flatbread she knew Evie had brought. Conversations between Tae and Evie operated on two levels, with two purposes: one, conversational – to keep things seeming normal in front of other people. It was like a game. You could never be quite sure what the other message was, only that there was one underneath. Before Tae and Mike got together, Evie and Mike had coffee together on weekends and sometimes visited at each other's houses. Half of Mike's church seemed to come to see them dance at the summer festival and when she asked Mike about it, he said Tae, did you see how many people were there?

Tae listened to Mike talking about people she didn't know. She felt like she was just visiting. People from the club seemed obsessed with rock and roll. They all started sentences with 'Oh at the club . . .' Evie caught her eye.

'Ever think of joining the club, Tae?' She took a sip of wine, which looked cold and crisp. Tae and Evie both knew this was just polite conversation. People had suggested Tae join before, but how could she? Her partner was already taken. And Tae wasn't about to fool herself into thinking she'd ever be a dancer.

'Not really my thing. I'm not the most coordinated person.' Something got lodged in Tae's throat, as if to prove her point and she coughed. Tae hated Evie's casual question about the club but worse than that, she'd let on it bothered her. They went on eating. The clink of their forks on the plates.

'Enjoying it out here?' Evie asked.

'Yeah, thanks. Nice area.' There was a pause. Tae was starting to feel wound up. 'It's nice.'

'Have you discovered the new Malaysian yet?'

'Yeah, Mike and I went last weekend, so good.'

That was a lie – they'd walked past – but when she told Evie yes, Evie said 'cool' and Tae felt validated somehow, while wanting Evie to know she and Mike went out for romantic dinners.

'Where's, um, sorry, I've forgotten your partner's name.'

Evie forked up some beetroot salad. 'Ryan.'

Tae reached for another piece of bread, the last piece, and tore it in half. 'What's Ryan up to?'

Evie shrugged. 'Probably gone home to have a shower and get changed.' They'd run aground. She may as well have said she assumed he was out meeting someone for a quick fuck. But then she said, 'He's on nights at work,' and Tae remembered he did shift work.

When she was able to, Tae went to stand in a corner with Naomi and Pete, Naomi's boyfriend. Naomi and Tae talked, but only to each other, not to Pete. Tae struggled to focus as she was always looking for where Evie was in relation to them. Naomi let out a sigh and said, 'You know statistically, moving in with your partner is the worst thing you could do for your sex life.'

'Couldn't you just pretend to like it?' Pete said.

'I've been free from the bondage of pleasing men for,

um, about twenty years,' said Naomi, smiling at Tae. Pete was tall and broad shouldered, with a shapely cock, which did a lot of pleasing Naomi, according to Naomi. Tae nursed her lemonade, wondering if he meant the sex or the house. Outside, the kids were having a dance competition.

'Who are all these people?' Naomi said.

Tae cleared her throat. 'I don't really know. I mean, I know who they are. From the club, mostly.'

Evie was talking to Mike now, throwing her head back and laughing a lot.

Tae whispered, 'Look at them,' and Naomi nodded.

'Don't you think Mike would worry about God's retribution too much to have an affair?' Naomi said to Tae. 'Or maybe he's testing the waters.' Naomi took the whole lapsed Christian thing a bit far.

Tae sat there for ages, even after Naomi, having drunk perhaps too many beers, started arguing with Pete. Even after Shane told Mike that the chicken kebabs looked undercooked, and he wouldn't be having any. Every now and then, Tae pretended to look at her phone, but mostly she just sat there.

Just Evie's presence was enough to make Tae lose her balance. And that laugh. Everyone liked Evie.

Mike and Evie were still talking. Evie's hand was resting on Mike's shoulder and Evie turned around to look at Tae. She just left her hand there and there was nothing good about that moment and there was nothing Tae could do to change it. And for a longer moment Tae gave them such a look, her eyebrows raised, till Mike stepped back, surprised and everyone went quiet.

Later Tae found Evie outside. She was talking to Kath, who was leaving to pick up her daughter from soccer. When Kath had gone, the two of them kept standing there at the picnic table, dipping crackers into a big bowl of hummus. Tae could hear the crunch of the crackers between their teeth. Say it, say it, Tae thought. I saw you over there. Flirting away. It would be a relief to go all out, telling it like it was. If only she could have a couple of wines. Evie had drunk two full glasses of sav blanc at lunch and was onto her third.

'So, what about you, Evie?' She heard herself saying it. 'What is it you want?'

'What do you mean, Tae?' Tae's question had surprised her, but only slightly. She sounded a bit drunk.

'We all want things, don't we?' Tae gathered herself. 'In a general sense, I mean?' Tae didn't mention Mike. She tried to regain control of whatever it was she was losing. Evie wouldn't have any idea what she meant.

'Well, apart from the obvious . . . making the regionals in July with Mike.'

Tae smiled. 'Yeah, obviously.'

'That's pretty much all I'm thinking about right now, to be honest.'

I bet you are, Tae thought.

Tae started clearing away people's glasses. Mike came out, then followed her into the kitchen, apologising, not waiting to see if Evie would join or notice.

'What was going on there?' Tae said, as lightly as she could manage. 'She makes her presence felt, doesn't she?' She moved from the sink to the fridge, like he wasn't there. On the kitchen counter, a knife and cleaver were neatly laid out beside the meat carcass. The blood had been washed off and the knife put away, but there were still a few slices left on the chopping board.

'I think we've had a way of relating to each other for so long now . . . it's taking a bit of an adjustment, for her maybe.

And you know Ev, she's super friendly with everyone.'

Something rose up in Tae. She stared at the cleaver. 'You might want to stop calling her Ev.' She picked up a chocolate chip biscuit instead and bit into it. 'I see the way you look at her.' There was something that felt like thirst in the back of Tae's throat.

'I don't look at her in any way, Tae.'

'You're such a shit liar, Mike.' She was trying so fucking hard and he couldn't see it.

'What?' asked Mike. 'I'm not allowed to look at other women now?'

'You two are in something. Now isn't the time to be having this conversation.' She didn't trust herself to say what she really meant. He was meant to be better than this. 'Just go.' Mike sighed and walked out of the kitchen, saying something she didn't catch. He was exhausted from it, from convincing her he'd told her everything there was to know. Mike, she knew, was losing patience. For the moment, the kitchen was empty – apart from the pile of dirty dishes, half a bottle of rosé on the bench and plates wrapped in foil. Party leftovers. The rosé was the good stuff. Drinking was one of the few things she was extremely good at. With an unsteady hand, she picked up the cleaver and brought it down on a bit of meat.

When she turned around, there was a man standing there, smiling at her with crinkled up eyes. He had a good build and dark hair trimmed short and was holding a bike helmet.

'And you're . . . ?'

'Ryan.'

'Evie's husband.'

'Yeah,' he said. 'I think I'm late.'

There was something familiar about his voice. The weight of the Evie argument was still hanging thick in the air. She wondered if he could feel it too. He looked around the kitchen.

'Got your work cut out for you with this place.'

Tae nodded, taking in the unpainted gib, watching the sunlight filter through the old blinds to claim their space on the floorboards. Right now, she'd give anything for her old life back.

'How are you?'

'I'm good, thanks.' She coughed into her hand. 'How are you?'

'Yeah, fine. Just finished work. Hey, I was really sorry to hear about – you know.'

Tae stared at him. How could he know unless Mike had told Evie, or had Kath told her? Tae wondered what else she didn't know.

Evie came into the kitchen, hardly a few metres away, and he ducked back in the doorway.

'We need a few more cups,' Evie said, smiling too widely at Tae. She'd put on a sparkly cardigan over her T-shirt and the fabric was straining slightly over her breasts. Tae could smell her perfume. Tae got some cups down and handed them to Evie. Ryan didn't move. He had to be kidding. 'Thanks,' Evie said and walked back down the hallway to the lounge.

Tae laughed. 'Hiding from your wife?' She tried to sound casual. Ryan frowned when she said that which made her wonder if he disliked being reminded that he was married. Like there was a problem.

'Can I borrow your bike?' Tae said. She wasn't sure what she'd expected Evie's husband to look like, somehow not like this. She undid the tie in her hair and shook her head, letting her hair tumble down around her ears.

He looked surprised. 'What do you want it for?'

'I just need some fresh air, that's all,' Tae said, over the conversation already. She couldn't really be bothered trying to flirt with him. She pulled on her gumboots, and he followed her as she cut through the garden to the other side. The overgrown lawn extended into a rectangular shape to a corrugated-iron fence. She could still hear the party. There were four bikes leaning against the fence.

'Take that one,' he said, pointing to a BMX. It was a burgundy frame, with gold handlebars. She could tell the seat was too low, so she raised it. She didn't ask who it belonged to.

'Do you mind if I join you? Could do with some more fresh air.' He got on an old-looking ten-speed. She hadn't invited him, but whatever. She'd done well inside, lasting that long. She might even stay out all day. As long as he didn't expect a conversation.

They pushed the bikes over to the gate that led to the river. The wind was picking up and she thought about getting her jacket, but it felt too hard to go back. There was power in leaving. They went right at the gate and rode up onto the river path towards the bridge. A man biked past, a pit bull running behind him. It was meant to be on a lead. The houses on this side were set low, lower than the path. Mike's house was in the tsunami risk zone, the portion of the coast coloured bright red on the map. It was why the house was cheap. The bike seat was still a bit low, but Tae kept going, concentrating on the track, swerving around potholes. They rode in single file, her in front. The smoke from the factory across the river coiled up and disappeared into the air. They rode past the kindergarten. The swings in the playground were moving slightly in the wind. Ryan came up so they were parallel.

There was nobody else out here. The concrete pillars of the train bridge cast shadows over the water. There was fresh white paint over the graffiti on the underpass. Keep going, she told herself. Ryan was further up ahead now. She pushed on, her legs beginning to ache. But she was liking being out here. Maybe he didn't want anything. Anyway, it didn't matter. Tae pushed the bike onto the bridge. From here you got a view down to where the river met the harbour. Crossing the bridge would mean surrendering to the wind. Something rattled and she nearly changed her mind and went back. This probably was a bad idea. There were some kids playing basketball on one of the hard courts on the other side. She almost missed the noise of the party, talking to Naomi. She hadn't intended to bike up this far. She wondered about the choices she'd made and what she could do. Ryan was off his bike at the far side. He was dropping stones down into the water, but when he saw her he raised his hand to wave her over. She pushed the bike over and leaned it against the bridge, then stood with her elbows resting on the top. With his face damp and hair flattened he seemed less sure of himself than he had at the house.

'Trouble in paradise?'

Did he know anything? What did he know?

'Oh,' she said like she hadn't really thought about it. She stared at him, wondering where that had come from. 'No.' But it was more like a question. She hadn't expected to find him attractive. Since the miscarriage she'd felt nothing. Mike had been understanding, but she missed the connection as much as the slow, lazy fucking that left them sleepy and relaxed.

'I'll show you something,' he said, heading over to where the guardrail ended. She could see what he was heading towards –

a ledge jutting out beneath the bridge. 'You'll love it.'

'I can see the river from here, thanks.' The clouds were grey and fast now. Rain later, maybe.

'Come on. It's much better from here.' He climbed down towards the ledge.

'What if a train comes?' She walked over, wishing again that she had her jacket.

'They don't run on the weekends.' He waited for her as she clambered down. There was a big space underneath the bridge, a bit like a stage. There was a strange, industrial feeling and the back wall was scribbled on with graffiti.

'See, you're fine.'

She nodded. If you say so.

They sat on the floor, a few metres back from the ledge. They were out of the wind now. It was dark under there, making the river appear much brighter. She didn't look at him. Maybe she couldn't trust Mike because she didn't trust herself. How could she trust herself when her body had failed her? While the miscarriage was unexpected, it didn't scare Mike in the way it scared her. The thing about Mike was he considered things, thought things through.

'Do you usually leave your own parties?' He laughed. Evie should be so lucky, Tae thought. His expression seemed to say *should I be worried?* But she was probably projecting.

'Things are complicated.' She didn't want to know about him, or even how it felt to kiss him.

'Wait until you have kids. Oh shit, sorry.' He made a face. 'It's the dirty laundry, the day-to-day, mundane work weeks,' he said. 'I think that's why Evie dances, to forget all that for a bit.'

Everything Tae wanted to ask seemed off limits. 'What about you? What do you do to forget?'

It sounded like a come on. 'I mean, what are you into?' Not much better.

She couldn't stay out here forever.

'I have to go.' It was abrupt, but she didn't care. She stood up and started climbing back up the bank.

They emerged up into the grey light and pushed the bikes the rest of the way over the bridge. They rode past the old macrocarpa trees, up over the stop bank next to the golf course. The second bridge was further up. Back across the river was the line of lit-up houses, including theirs somewhere. Had moving in with Mike just been the easiest option? She couldn't afford to buy a house. The river was higher here, where it met the incoming tide. She had never been up this far before. The bike skidded in the gravel before she managed to right it again. She kept going and didn't turn around. Tomorrow she would get the bus into town and meet Naomi for lunch on the waterfront, like they used to. Her shoulder was starting to hurt now, tight, and achy. It hadn't been this hard on the way up.

The lights were on in the kitchen, and she could see Naomi at the window and Mike's head bent over his phone. No sign of Evie. The driveway was empty of cars.

'Can I ask you something, Tae?'

'Yeah.' They leaned the bikes against the back fence.

'Is anything going on between Mike and Ev? Like other than dance stuff?' He was uncomfortable.

Tae hesitated, as though she'd forgotten something, then undid the strap on her helmet.

'Some of us actually live monogamous lives, you know,' she said. It wasn't really an answer, and meaner than she'd intended, but it was all she had.

'Good to know,' Ryan said. They walked towards the house. 'I'll pick up Evie's bike tomorrow.'

Tae opened the front door, then kicked her gumboots off.

'You disappeared,' said Naomi. She pulled Tae down onto the two-seater. 'Want some coffee?'

Tae's knees hurt. 'Yeah, please. I just needed to get out for a bit.'

She looked at Mike. 'Ryan asked me if there was anything going on with you two. I couldn't give him a straight answer.'

She spread her fingers over the coffee cup, warming them. That was going nowhere. 'Shall we do some sorting? Go through some of those boxes? Nomes won't mind, will you?'

'I don't mind.'

They sat on the sofa while Mike dragged in the boxes. Tae pulled out an orange road cone. They all looked at it. Then Tae took out a fabric lamp. She ran her fingers down the length of it, then held it out to Naomi. 'Are you sure?' Naomi held up the lamp. It had an hourglass shape and wooden base.

Scarce Objects

Hana waited until low tide, when she was able to cross back over the mud flats to the house. When the land drained, the cable roots underneath the house were visible. Some pencil-like, others cone-shaped, sticking up through the rotting decking. Criss-crossed vines swelled the drains, and the foundations seemed to be collapsing under the weight of the trees. But Hana wasn't thinking about the state of the house. She was thinking about tides and wind direction and reclaiming what was theirs. In the city, she'd been down to the bar on the wharf and met excited pale-faced men there who would be perfect.

When she got to the house, she took off her mud-encrusted boots. The steps to the front door crackled with dead leaves and the windows were coated in a thick layer of salt. Everything was the colour of setting concrete.

Belle was sprawled out on a grubby-looking mattress on the porch, holding her nose. She was new and wasn't used to things yet and everywhere was this smell, a cross between river sewage and shellfish. Miri and Wai were in the back kitchen sorting the kāpia, ready for boiling down. When the kauri trees started coming down the women used the kauri gum to make useful items. They needed to do something.

'You're back,' Belle said, eyeing Hana up from underneath her thick fringe.

'No shit.' Hana sprinkled water on her hands before

coming into the porch. 'And you're doing nothing again, I see.'

Belle made a face. 'I thought you weren't talking to me.'

Hana knew Belle was already itching to be gone. That she'd heard about the city, where there were clubs; where they served mataī beer in tall glasses and the dialect was different. She wanted to go there, she'd told Hana. They'd had an argument. Hana said if any of them ever took that road, they'd have lost right there, and that Belle had better work a lot faster if she was ever going to go anywhere. Belle had spat a pale gold ball of kāpia on the wooden floor.

'The wind's picking up,' Hana said. 'Not that you'll be remotely interested, Belle.'

'What happened at the wharf?' Wai yelled from in the back. 'Any sign of Angel?'

Angel was Wai's cousin, who used to live with them. Belle stood up and followed Hana out of the porch into the kitchen.

'Unfortunately, no Angel,' said Hana. She missed Angel. It was mean of her to disappear like that from the last house, whoever the man was. Hana hoped it wouldn't last.

In the kitchen, a large wooden table was covered with nubs and chips of kāpia, the kauri gum piled roughly according to size. Wai was standing at one end surveying the collection, Miri was at the sink. 'But I talked to some men. I let one of them buy me a drink.'

As a general rule they didn't approach strangers, but last week Hana told the women what they already knew; the objects were becoming scarce. 'We've given up things, had to,' she'd said. 'There needs to be a balancing—we need something in return.'

Miri put a large pot in the sink and turned on the tap. The water often came out tinged with algae, or swarming with tadpoles, which they collected and put in saucepans to grow. 'Woah. And?'

'They talked in fast, strange accents, but I picked up enough to make sense. He said he'd been a sailor but not anymore. He was going to work at a place called The Colony.'

'The Colony? What's that?' Belle laughed, looking at the ornaments carved from kāpia on the shelf: a gum teapot with a little gum cup, an elaborately carved gum head.

'It's a place where the driving dams help float kauri, the only buoyant native timber, *didn't I know*.' Hana rolled her eyes. 'When water is released from behind the dam, the logs *cascade* – get this, he really said that – downstream with it.'

'Let's bait them,' Wai said, holding up a piece of kāpia the size of her fist. 'Make something happen. That kauri doesn't belong to them.'

'He said where he comes from there isn't any of this beautiful wood, with its fine grain.' Hana had smiled: let him believe this was new information to her. He smiled back and said he was lucky to be going to work for a man called Henry Sallow.

*

That night, the women formed a plan, even Belle agreeing that Hana knew best. Hana would go to The Colony, and she would talk to the men. There had to be a way to restore things.

The tide was out when she put on her boots and went down the steps and across the mud flats. It was a half day's walk to the wharf and from there she would find Sallow. The sun was high in the sky and there wasn't a breath of wind. Later, they'd wonder how they'd missed the signs something terrible was coming.

When she got back the next morning she wasn't like their Hana. There was no raucous laughter, no banging of doors. She lay down in her room, her mouth moving without any sound. It was her face, but it was blank. Wai clocked the bruising around her thighs and wrists, and nudged Miri, pointing at Hana's feet. Hana still had her boots on.

'What's going on?' Miri asked.

Hana pretended not to hear, turned her face to the wall. Belle was standing in the doorway.

'Why have you got your boots on inside, Hana?' Belle said. 'That's a filthy habit.'

'Men,' Miri said, pointing to the blood on Hana's shorts.

'Bringing all the dirt inside,' Belle said.

'Shut up, Belle,' said Wai.

Belle shrugged, but they could see fear in her eyes. Not because of the tone in Wai's voice, but because of what the men had done to Hana.

'We've let things slide,' Wai said. 'And this is the result.'

It was silent for what felt like a long time. Wai started to mutter under her breath, then it became a hum. Quiet at first, gradually getting louder until Miri started singing the song with Wai, and Belle, relieved she knew the words, joined in too.

*

When Wai appeared on Angel's verandah, Angel stared at her, not understanding at first. But her voice turned low and frantic and Angel knew Wai was telling the truth about Hana. It had taken Wai two days to find Angel, and she was dirty and tired. Angel couldn't stand to think of those men hurting Hana, or Wai or anyone.

'Let's go,' she said. Hana had been good to her when she had lived with the women. And nobody had told Angel what living with a man would be like.

She hadn't exactly noticed the sick worry in her stomach, but as she and Wai approached the house, Angel noticed it was gone. She knew Wai still hadn't forgiven her for disappearing, but Hana's situation seemed to have forced her into a state of acceptance.

They crossed the mud flats and Belle came out onto the porch, chewing something. 'So this is the famous cousin we've heard so much about.'

It was Angel's first time here. Inside, she couldn't keep her focus in one place; her eyes darted around the room as she absorbed the details. There were portrait photographs on the wall, some people Angel recognised, faded black-and-white in assorted frames. A gun lay dismantled on the bench beside a can of oil, the bits laid out neatly, a rare sign of order. There were twisted rags everywhere.

'How long have you been here?' Angel asked.

'Few months,' said Miri, exhaling. 'But it feels like forever.'

The collection had overtaken the house, spilling out of the back room and onto the porch. Wooden shelves lined the walls of every room, some of them bowing under the weight of the objects. Angel walked about, looking at everything, picking up the occasional item. She ran a finger around the inside of a tuatara jawbone. A bat skeleton embedded in limestone lay next to a possum skull. Bigger items were stored on the verandah, under the corrugated-iron roof. A moa skeleton assembled from stray bones stood beside two skeletons of kurī.

The item Angel loved the most was kept in a carved

wooden box beside Hana's mattress. No matter what house they had been in, Hana made sure the box was right there. Angel was younger than the others and always asked Hana if she could see it before she went to bed. In the night, there was the crackle and bark of branches moving in the wind, the call of a ruru, the rustle of things hiding. Hana always sighed, but she would open the box – it was something she could do. 'Remember you're only here because you're Wai's cousin,' she would say.

Inside the box, the kauri-gum hair was a tress of silky blond. The gum had been melted, spun into threads, then plaited while warm and tied with a ribbon.

Now she was back, there were things Angel wanted to tell the others: they needed to know the men were the same everywhere. But Hana didn't need to hear that. What happened to Hana had changed everything. They were all together; Wai said that was all that mattered.

Hana and Miri stood at the stove, in front of a large pot, and Wai and Belle sat at the big table. Angel was standing, watching Hana. Hana's hair was matted with salt, and she had bite marks on her neck.

'Hana,' said Angel, but it was Wai who got up from the table and came over.

'One of those days,' Miri said, 'when you're about to give up and then everything falls into place. Check it out.' Angel pretended she hadn't noticed the state Hana was in, but nobody was fooled.

'War wounds,' Wai said, bumping her knuckles against Angel's chin as she passed.

'Do you know what this is?' Miri asked.

Hana jerked her head up and peered over the steam. Miri

held up a scrap of metal. There was a depression in it, a glassy substance inside.

'It's the lead from the ship out on the mudflats.' It wasn't surprising Hana knew what it was. Hana had been collecting for years. Hana was a doer. And now Hana was unravelling.

Miri shrugged. 'Strange, looks like tītī fat inside.' She dropped the lead and reached out her right arm to lean on the bench beside it.

'I thought this meeting was urgent?' Belle said. 'Wai?' As soon as it was high tide, Angel and Wai needed to leave to find Sallow.

Wai ignored Belle, but picked up a stick, and dipped it into the pot. 'Okay, so we need to remind ourselves why we're doing this.'

She twirled the kāpia around the stick then squashed it onto the bench. Angel tried to see what she was making. Then Wai picked off a small cube of the soft, hot gum and dropped it back into the pot. She paused, then held up the melted-down cube, which she then mangled into something—a little figure of some sort. Angel realised it was a kāpia doll Hana with a little black hat and black boots. As Wai talked, she danced the kāpia Hana from side to side.

'Hana went down to Sallow's to talk,' she said.

Hana's head jerked up again at the mention of her name, and her eyes moved back and forth with the kāpia Hana.

'She told them this is our home,' Wai said. 'She suggested they arrange a meeting, invite everyone. It was no longer working, she said, things could be lost. Maybe had been already. But the men had secured a big job, and every one of them was out of their mind on whisky.'

Hana brought her hands up, clasping them behind her neck. Her eyes didn't leave the kāpia Hana.

'Kept going on about their patch of paradise,' Wai said. 'When she tried to leave, they wouldn't let her.' She cleared her throat. 'Grim. Not Hana. Not a chance in hell we could let that go on.'

Wai dipped more gum into the pot and began working on it.

'I'm making taki,' Wai said. 'You know what they are?'

Angel shook her head.

'Kind of like a decoy. For you and Wai when you go. The kāpia protects us.'

'It didn't protect Hana though,' Angel said, in a low voice.

'There wasn't one for Hana when she went to Sallow's,' Wai said.

A noise came from Hana's throat.

Wai shuddered and turned the stick between her fingers. 'We got complacent. None of us are invincible.'

'You'll take a taki doll each with you,' Miri said to Angel and Wai. 'These men have to own their mistakes, to live with them.'

When the tide came in, Angel and Wai got ready. Wai dressed Angel in blue dungarees like her own, and a coarse grey shirt, a clasp-knife in her belt. She tied Angel's taki doll around her neck and put her own in her pocket. Wai was small, but thick with muscle. She could easily pass for a man. They had the same nose, but Angel was more girly, with her full mouth and hair down to her shoulder blades. When Hana had suggested she cut it, Angel shook her head.

'Your looks aren't going to protect you,' Hana told her.

Angel pulled out the taki doll necklace she was wearing, so it was on the outside of her dungarees. With its golden kāpia face, hard black boots and jaunty hat, it looked ready. Hana nodded.

It took a few moments for their eyes to adjust to the darkness. The salt water was right up under the house now. Wai pulled the rope attached to the boat and Angel climbed in. It felt good to be on the water again. Wai grabbed her paddle. The lanes were narrow and winding, walled with mangroves, and could be difficult to navigate until you got out on the river. It would be light in a couple of hours.

For a long time, there was nothing at all except mangroves. Angel didn't sing, but Wai kept singing for longer than usual, her face illuminated by the torch strapped to the bow. The branches of ancient pōhutukawa bent down to scrape the water. There were golden kōwhai and trees laden with wild peaches. Against the narrow strip of sky visible, clouds collected then dispersed, and the deep blue began to lighten. Finally, there was an opening ahead, and they pulled clear of the trees and joined the outgoing tide. They lifted their paddles and drifted now, glad of a rest. They'd never seen anyone else out here, but sometimes they came across an abandoned raft or canoe. And Angel sometimes heard the voices of the drowned, although the others said she imagined it.

They passed over the heads of eels, tāmure and flounder. Angel saw other things too: fins and tails close to breaking the surface, then stretching and changing. They knew these paths of the sea and their changeable moods. And there were the ancient floating logs, which sometimes behaved in a disconcerting way. The estuary looked more like a wasteland, the huge, waterlogged kauri trees floating and bumping along as far as the eye could see.

They left the boat tied to an old pūriri at the edge of the

mangroves and climbed onto the nearest tree trunk. They could walk from here. Even though the tide had turned, it seemed to Angel that nothing was moving, that their walking towards the harbour made no difference to where they were. The logs underfoot had ridges in circular patterns; it felt like walking over bones. They didn't talk, going in single file. It was safer that way. Miri had misjudged a log once and slipped down. Her foot had been crushed, and it took a long time to work her free.

The Colony glittered in white isolation in a clearing of bush near the wharf. Henry Sallow's day-to-day business was cabinets and dining tables, but his house imitated the Taj Mahal, even set on a raised plinth with four towering minarets. It was built from kauri and the dome on the top was covered in marble. Dozens of smaller, prefabricated Taj Mahal models for keeping meat and tobacco fresh were stacked outside the sawmill. Wai laughed when she saw them. She told Angel that at lunchtime the staff would fish off the ramp – often catching so many tāmure they were thrown to the dogs or left to rot.

The walls of the mill were hung with every crosscut saw you could imagine, teeth shaped like miniature finials. Freshly sawn kauri logs were stacked tightly everywhere and there were two new-looking boats, half-painted. The ground in the yard was smooth, flattened by the men's boots coming and going, in and out.

Angel squatted and pissed on a stack of pallets, the hard light of day on her face. The cicadas were deafening, like a warning. Sallow was in the yard, working on the prefabs. He had his back to them. Two other men were sawing a log nearby, using a crosscut saw. It was making a loud vibration.

Wai gave her a look to tell her: Now. She pulled her dungarees up then unbuttoned the top two buttons on her shirt. May as well use it. The hat of the taki doll was just visible. She waited, hidden, the side of the knife digging into her thigh.

Wai whistled, and when Sallow turned in her direction his face was the colour of eggshell.

'What can I do for you?' he asked, as though he was trying to remember his manners. But when Wai stuck out her hand he struggled to smile.

'Forgive my intrusion,' Wai said, 'but it seems you've been taking something that's not yours.'

'We're about to stop for lunch. No point hanging around. I suggest you go home or come back later.'

Home. In the shadows, Angel tried the word out on her tongue. The way he said it, it sounded unfamiliar.

'Everything you see here is pre-ordered. First day of next week the next flotation of kauri will be ready—panelling, sarking, architraves.'

Angel arranged her hair so it fell in the front, and walked out into view. Sallow looked at her hair and unbuttoned shirt and down at her legs, as if he owned her. Men like Sallow were always saying that she had stolen things, which was the wrong way around.

He walked towards her.

'How old are you?' Like it mattered. His stomach was right there, where his grey shirt parted from the belt of his pants.

The vibration from the crosscut saw stopped.

One of the men said 'Right goer' and the other laughed. But Angel was long past caring about insults like these.

Sallow looked at her as though she'd never known anything in her life and never wanted to.

'We're looking for work,' she said.

Wai stood watching. The Hana taki doll was sticking out of her side pocket. Its little black hat had slipped down, almost over its eyes.

Sallow smiled at Angel, long and slow. He unbuttoned his shirt, damp with sweat and took it off, dropping it on the ground. A flock of tūturiwhatu sounded from above.

'I'll take whatever you have going. I learn quickly. I could help with the Taj Mahal.'

He laughed and turned his body away, stacking the last of the wood. The yard was empty now – the others had gone for their lunch. She watched the birds, their increasing cries a distraction. They were circling, low.

'Nobody works on that except me.'

'Bet you've never been to the original. Too busy making prefabs.' Angel circled him too, waiting, counting. From miles away, inside the walls of the mangroves, came a chorus. For an instant, she saw Hana, Miri and Belle standing at the kāpia pot. The doll felt hot against her chest. 'You're stealing our wood.'

A tūturiwhatu landed nearby on the stack of timber. It made eye contact with her, and that was all Angel needed. She felt for the knife at her waist.

'You know what you look like? A scared rāpeti.' She laughed, screwing up her nose. 'You've taken the wood, so we need something in return.'

A rash climbed up Sallow's doughy neck, all pink and white. He pulled out a handkerchief and rubbed it over his face. Then, with thick white fingers, he lit a cigarette and leaned against a chair stacked with rubbish.

The knife glimmered as she removed it. 'Sorry,' said Angel. Wai was standing up now, ready. 'But it's not like you haven't done worse.'

In one movement Wai pinned Sallow's hand to the chair. A bead of sweat ran down his nose onto his lip. He seemed paralysed, then after a moment he started to pray. He was wasting his breath. She had imagined being slow and deliberate, but one good push through and it was done. When she held the finger up, it was already changing colour. It left a dark shape of itself where it had bled onto the chair. She wrapped the bloody finger in the shirt Sallow had dropped on the ground.

*

When Angel and Wai returned, everyone gathered around the table. They took out their taki dolls and laid them on the table, side by side. Angel offered up her finds, from foraging out on the mangroves and down at the wharf. She saved the finger till last, unfolding the crumpled-up shirt. Hana and Miri leaned in, their arms folded. 'It's his,' Angel said. She passed it to Hana. Angel wasn't sorry. These past days, Hana had been so altered. Hana grabbed it, and for a moment it was like they were having a wordless conversation.

'We need some hair from everyone before the sun goes down,' Hana said.

Angel was too tired to argue. Only Belle complained she was growing hers out, but she lined up behind Wai and Miri and Angel. Hana got a knife and sliced off a lock from everyone. She sent Angel to fetch the kauri gum hair from her room.

Hana unravelled the braid into its three separate strands. Then she wove in the thick black strands of the women's hair. The result was stunning: a black-and-gold zigzag six-strand braid.

Hana slid the finger inside the braid. They set the whole thing in kāpia, attaching the lead from the old ship as base using the tītī fat and a stingray tooth. The women worked on it all night, in candlelight, in silence. They moved from the stove only to follow the patch of moonlight on the floor. Once it was done, Hana put it over Angel's head and Angel fell asleep.

When the dawn light came in the window, Hana was there beside her. Angel pulled the necklace away from her body so they could see what they had made. They stared at it, taking in its power. If this worked, the wood might be recoverable too.

The others woke and moved silently around the kitchen, setting down plates for breakfast. Their faces turned to Angel, who looked exhausted, yet in her eyes was a kind of power. She wore the necklace, watching the women notice it, gaze at it.

Everyone sat down to eat.

The Game

'He came into my room this morning in just a towel.' Remi empties the food scraps into the compost bin, then puts the lid back on it. Her feet are bare and filthy. She and Jade have been building the chicken hut all day.

Jade bends down to pick a stone out of the freshly turned soil which is dusty and browny grey. She stares at the stone, then closes her hand over it.

'I thought you said he was hot.' Her voice is meaner than she intended. When he'd opened the front door of the flat just moments ago, she felt a pull in her body. Lewis. A mouth she'd like to kiss. Short dark hair and dark eyes.

'He works at a school for emotionally disturbed kids. He sometimes has to restrain them.' Remi looks at her muddy hands. 'And he's a Sagittarius. We're going to the Tate next week.' Remi is a Gemini and Jade is a Virgo.

The last boyfriend Jade had was an Aquarius. 'Two overthinkers. You won't have an easy sexual relationship.' They'd lasted a month. That was a year ago and Jade's only been on two Tinder dates since, both awful.

Jade pulls her ponytail higher onto her head then smooths out her fringe. She only helped Remi move in here two weeks ago. This is Jahna and Tom's place. They're Jade's friends from work at the art studio. They had two rooms up for rent. Remi moved into one. Lewis answered the ad in the wholefood store window and moved into the other.

But Jade already knows how it ends. She's known Remi longer than she hasn't known her. Every time Remi breaks up with someone, she moves in with Jade, sometimes for days, sometimes for weeks. Jade's flat is on the other side of the park and is tiny.

Lewis comes around the corner of the house pushing a wheelbarrow full of rubble. He's tall, and a bit of a tattoo is poking out of his shirt sleeve. The courtyard is filled with yucca plants, and ceramic pots in varying sizes line the wall, some with plants, some waiting to be filled. Remi makes a show of pointing out the new flower beds to Jade, while fiddling with the strap on her vest top, letting it fall off her shoulder. The mounds of dirt side by side remind Jade of freshly dug graves. Lewis parks the wheelbarrow so it's parallel with the fence and turns to face them.

'Tom said this was a bomb site back in the day. Explains all the rubble,' he says. There's a spot above the corner of his lips, like a beauty spot that people sometimes draw on with eyeliner. It could be dirt.

Remi laughs like he's said something hilarious. She walks over to the tomato plants held up with stakes in a neat row.

'We should jump the fence at the Lido when it gets dark,' she says. The Lido is the local outdoor pool, across the road from the flat. 'Except Jade won't come. She hates the Lido.'

Jade feels her cheeks go hot. She says, 'I should just get over it.' They're both looking at her and waiting so she tells the story as fast as she can. She's no good at this, despite having told it a few times over the years. It's like Remi's decided Jade's the entertainment.

'South London breaststroke final and I'm up against this girl from Dulwich, Ines Khan. It was a false start, but I got to the halfway rope and threw it off.' She laughs, surprising herself. 'I thought they were trying to stop me winning.'

He laughs and she laughs again, with him.

'How old were you?' Lewis says.

'Fifteen.'

'The stadium totally loved it, they cheered and cheered,' Remi says, and twists off a ripe tomato. 'She had to swim again. She loved it too.'

Jade can only remember the laughter while she walked back the length of the pool in her clingy, wet swimsuit. Remi is looking at Lewis staring at Jade and the energy is weird and the sun burns overhead. He bends down and turns on the tap by the compost bin. He splashes his face with water, then uses his arm to dry his face. The beauty mark is still there.

'Please tell me this ends well,' he says.

Remi picks up a bamboo stake leaning against the fence and jams it into the ground.

'She won,' Remi says.

Later, Jade and Lewis sit at a table in the courtyard drinking with Jahna and Tom. Remi's not drinking – 'just to try it out, for a bit,' she told Jade. She's grilling vegetables on the barbecue at the end of the table and has changed into a top that she's wearing like a minidress. Jahna's telling Lewis about the veggie co-op they belong to. The smoke rises up and drifts over the trees as though the city has taken a breath. The sky has dimmed to a deep blue and a few stars are appearing. People start arriving, with plates and pots full of food, which they put on the table. There aren't enough seats, so some people sit on the lawn. At the table, plates are passed around and people fill them with food.

'Wow, that okra.' Remi is on Jade's left, at the head of the table. The vodka's gone to Jade's head. She takes a bite of okra, then another. Lately she's been too tired to cook for herself, picking up ready meals from the station on the way home.

'I hope you've all got your tickets for the festival,' Remi says.

Jade says, 'I'm on the morning shift Saturday.'

She helps at the co-op on the weekends. During the week she works at the art studio. It covers her rent, but she needs to figure something else out soon.

'Can't you swap with someone?'

Remi gets an allowance from her parents. She works, but part-time, at a boutique store. Something touches Jade's leg under the table, and she shifts slightly. There's a hand on her knee now, not moving. Remi wouldn't, would she?

The game started when they were ten or eleven. They called it Nuts and Bolts and they played it in the basement while Remi's parents were upstairs. Remi would always decide the order of things when they played the game. Remi usually chose Jade to be the victim. The rules were no talking or eye contact. The rapist had to break through the door and pin the victim on the bed by the wrists and pull up their shirt and push down hard on their body. And say mean things. Jade always worried about being found out, but they never were. Recently, Jade found out that Remi's mum Anita had been raped around that time. She'd been shocked about the rape, but also about the fact that Remi didn't tell her at the time they played the game. It was, in fact, the whole reason they played the game. Remi was in therapy now and was working a lot of stuff out. By sharing her pain, she felt less pain.

'No partying for me either, school reports to write,' Lewis says. Both Remi's hands are visible. A finger strokes Jade's knee. Jade looks across at Lewis like she's noticing him for the first time again. She smiles at him, and he smiles back. Around them, the others are laughing and talking. She looks down at the rapidly cooling okra on her plate and stuffs two pieces into her mouth at once. Tom reaches past her for a basket of bread.

'Jahna and I are coming,' he says. 'There are some permaculture workshops this year.' Her skirt is slowly being pushed up her leg from the hem. Something strokes the inside of her thigh. She moves her foot, not a kick exactly, more of a nudge and the stroking stops. She kicks harder and this time he starts kicking her back. Someone knocks over a glass of wine and she hears him say, 'I'll go. I've got it,' and he stands up and leaves the table. A moment later she gets up and goes inside too. It's dark in the hall and he's standing on the stairs. She moves past him and their hips touch. He grabs her hand and laces his fingers into hers until they're tight. Then there's Remi's voice from downstairs asking if they want dessert.

The café is cool and dark, relief from the heat that feels like it's trying to submerge the city. Remi orders bubble tea. When the waiter brings them, Jade and Remi try them both and decide the white peach is the best. Remi slips out of her sandals and places her bare feet on the bench opposite.

'We played that crazy game where you sit on someone's shoulders and try to get the other person into the water. Oh.' She stands up and pulls a small envelope out of her skirt pocket, then pushes it across the table. 'He said to give you this.' Then she sits back down.

'He likes you. I can tell,' Jade says. She fingers the envelope. She has this feeling she sometimes gets, like she's a minor character in this play and Remi is the lead.

'Aren't you going to open it?'

Jade looks at Remi. She keeps looking at her.

'The seeds will go everywhere.'

Remi sucks the last of her bubble tea noisily through the straw.

'I better go pick up the car. I'm meeting the others in Croydon.'

'Got your licence?' Last year they caught the train out to the hire car place and Remi had left her driver's licence at home and had to go all the way back to get it. Jade doesn't drive. They'd got to the festival at midnight and the gates were closed and they slept in the car on the side of the road.

'Ha-ha very funny. Wish you were coming, Jadey.'

They say goodbye at the corner by the wholefood shop. Jade walks home slowly. The air is thick and close, and loud ska music is coming from a little stretch of park where the roads converge. She pulls the envelope out of her bag and opens it. Inside is a packet of seeds with a picture of a velvety crimson flower on the front. Nasturtium, Empress of India. A tiny folded-up bit of paper falls to the ground. She picks it up and unfolds it. *Call me.* And then his number.

She tries to wait, to run into him at the pub, but hasn't the patience. When she texts him, he replies straight away. It's his idea to meet at the Lido. *Cheeky fucker*, she texts back: although she can't be bothered thinking of anywhere else, she's just excited to hear from him. *Okay then*. She puts on a cotton sundress over last summer's red bikini.

He fingers her at the deep end of the pool, in the corner, against the ladder. He wants to fuck there, but there are swimmers in the next lane and there's the issue of the condom. Thankfully, the men's changing rooms are empty and they go into a cubicle at the end of the row. He takes her chin and tilts it towards his. As for what happens next, it isn't really a kiss. He is biting her lip and their teeth knock together and she is sure she tastes blood. For a moment she cannot breathe, but then their tongues establish contact. He pulls down his shorts and she starts to take off her bikini pants, but he turns her around so she's facing the wall and tells her to keep still. Her phone rings. She thinks about Remi while he rolls the condom on, then she thinks about nothing. Remi is at the festival. He pulls her pants to the side and gets deep inside her.

Afterwards, they walk to his and Remi's flat. The afternoon sun is baking. His bed is a futon on the floor, with fresh-looking white sheets and there is a big floor-to-ceiling window overlooking the park. There's nothing else in the room except for a stereo and a wooden clothes rail hung with clothes. They get into bed. He brings his face close to hers, then waits for her to kiss him. He doesn't initiate anything else, and she's partly hurt, and partly relieved. It felt familiar. It was like being with Remi. The feeling of someone having power over her, in a way that seems playful at first, but isn't, not really. She lies with her face in the pillow, and they fall asleep and when she wakes up the light has changed, but it is still light. She wants to have sex again, but Lewis is still asleep. She wraps a sheet around her body and goes into Remi's room and looks in the wardrobe. She chooses a gold silk top with long floaty sleeves she hasn't seen Remi wear before. She puts it on and looks at herself in the mirror. Her mouth looks swollen and sore. Out the window she can see the new flower beds, bordering the square patch of grass.

'The traffic on the M1 was backed up forever. We only just got the car back in time,' Remi says.

The longer Jade doesn't say anything about Lewis, the worse it's going to be when Remi finds out. But she wants to keep it to herself for a bit. She still smells of him. She and Remi are sitting at the kitchen table, drinking coffee, and flicking through their phones. The doors are open to the courtyard and sunlight is pouring into the kitchen.

'I texted him from the festival and told him to water the tomatoes and he sent a kiss back,' Remi says, and pours more coffee into her cup. 'The photos of the main stage are way better on my laptop.' They hear the front gate open, then someone coming up the side of the house. He's carrying a big cardboard box, so big only his lower body is visible. There are ventilation slits in the sides of the box.

'Chickens!' Remi says. 'Hello!' She gets up and goes outside. Jade stays where she is, on the chair, in the patch of sunlight, and pretends to look at her phone. She hears him say something, but she cannot hear all of it and then she hears the sound of the box being opened, maybe with a pocketknife.

Remi says, 'Jade, come and look.'

Jade goes outside and stands a little bit apart from them. Lewis takes the birds out of the box one at a time and puts them over the fence into the run. Two of the chickens have lost feathers and have bald patches on their heads and necks.

'Poor little things,' Jade says, staring at the birds.

He looks at her and nods. 'We'll sort them out, Jade. You planted those seeds yet?' He knows she hasn't.

'How are those reports going?' Jade says, but she's not into the joke, she can't keep this up much longer. She wants to have the conversation with Remi about the game.

Remi says, 'Yeah, how are those reports going, Lewis?' and goes inside to get her laptop.

He comes over to Jade and pins her there against the fence, his arms on either side of her. She can feel his hard stomach under his T-shirt. For the first time she doesn't need permission. She grabs his T-shirt in her hand and pulls him towards her. When she looks up at Remi's open bedroom window there is a movement, but she could be imagining it. She should move, but she doesn't. She kisses him, hard. Then she wipes her mouth with the back of her hand.

'What do you need to tell me?' Remi says, scattering the pellets. The dust from the pellets makes a blanket over the bird's feathers and then, when it shakes itself, forms tiny tracks in the dirt below.

They could talk about Lewis another time. Remi would cope. The sun is very hot.

Jade runs it through her head again. 'I wanted to talk to you. About the game.' Remi always initiated it.

'What game? The other one must be somewhere. Can you have a look?'

Jade unlatches the door of the chicken hut and peers into the darkness. 'It's here.' It doesn't move. She keeps looking at the bird until her eyes adjust. If it wasn't for its swollen claws and cloudy eyes, it could just as easily be sleeping.

'You were always getting me to play that Nuts and Bolts game.' She can't see Remi's face from here. It was the way they had always done it, that Jade was ready, whenever Remi initiated it.

Remi puts a container of water over the fence, knocking it sideways.

'It was nothing, Jade. We were kids.'

'I think it's dead.' Jade stands up and looks at Remi. 'It wasn't nothing though, was it?' She remembers the feeling of Remi's bed, the restraint of it.

'Gross!' Remi shakes her wrists up and down, splattering water on her shirt. She's hard to read sometimes, even after all these years. 'We didn't do anything wrong, Jade. It didn't mean anything.' She laughs.

'Why is everything a joke with you?' Jade considers the possibility that it meant something different to Remi, and now, faced with it, she doesn't know where to take it. 'It wasn't nothing.'

Remi shades her eyes with her hand. Her fingernails are painted a matte pink.

Jade says, 'If I'd known then, what had happened to your mum . . .'

Remi flinches. 'Don't put *that* on me, Jade. You didn't *have* to. You participated.'

'Maybe I didn't have it in me to say no. I was a *kid*.'

Remi wraps her arms tightly around her torso, like she's trying to keep herself warm. 'Why are you making me feel bad?' She's lost patience with whatever is going on here.

Jade picks up the bird and props it up on a shelf of branches, where, she hopes, the flies and ants will get to it first.

'That's stupid,' Remi says. 'Leave it. The other chickens will eat it. I saw it on a nature programme.'

When Jade turns around Remi is standing there. She seems to have made up her mind about something.

'It was my idea. Lewis didn't do anything to you that he doesn't do to me.' She grabs Jade's hand. 'Or did he restrain you?'

Jade stares at Remi, trying to figure out what she means. Neither of them says anything for a moment. What does she know? She knows.

Remi says, 'It was obvious you couldn't give him what he wanted.' She laughs. 'Poor Jadey.'

An ornate merry-go-round has been set up near the Herne Hill entrance to the park. A group of face-painted kids are waiting for it to open. Tents and stalls and parked vehicles line the main path up the hill. To the right is the main stage, covered in brightly coloured bunting and flags. A samba troupe in matching brown-and-gold T-shirts are keeping rhythm on the stage, their huge drums held against their bodies with wide red straps. The smell of jerk chicken is in the air. The crowd is already big, and it isn't even midday.

Further up the hill, past the Punch and Judy booth, are the fruit and vegetable sculptures. A scene from *King Kong*, made entirely from carrots, the cast from *Sesame Street*, a domestic violence scene entitled 'Arty Choke – it is never okay'. Boris Johnson, his deep purple tuxedo carved from an eggplant, with a pineapple collar and red capsicum skinny tie. Next is the main arena, where the sheep shearing and the Best in Show will be held. At three o'clock, a crowd will gather for the popular Flight of the Falcons display.

The jerk chicken stall is set up behind two parked trucks. The oven is a rusty 44-gallon drum turned on its side. A man stands behind it. He is wearing a green T-shirt with *Jamaica* on the front in yellow letters and a heavy-looking gold chain around his neck. He is turning the charred chicken with a pair of tongs and holding a water bottle in the other.

A bird man on stilts teeters past in a multi-coloured cloak of painted feathers and an elaborate headdress. He has enormous blue rubber hands, and he is waving them from side to side. A girl wearing a T-shirt that says *Bubble Inc.* on it is next, trailing a gigantic bubble behind her stretched out on a stick frame. A crowd of kids dance around her, mesmerised by the scale of it and the oily pinks and blues on its surface.

Remi and Lewis are standing in the Organic Produce arena, behind a wooden table covered in vegetables. There are people everywhere. Remi's wearing the gold silk top and looks very young, somehow. Lewis is talking and Remi looks like she is listening but she's not saying anything. He bends down and kisses her on the mouth. Jade slowly makes her way over between the tables and stops at the one next to them. She leans over, pretending to look at an eggplant. Remi comes over and stands in front of her and it's as though they're both holding their breath. Remi lifts her arms out, as though she's going to touch Jade and the sleeves on her top slide up her arms and there are marks on her wrists. She laughs. Then Lewis's arm is at Remi's waist, propelling her away, but she breaks free and merges with the crowd. A kid in a skeleton costume runs past, chasing a red balloon, but it must be helium because it goes up into the sky.

Mistaken

'All right, Neve? Feeling better?' a voice said from behind her. Neve swung her chair around as Rob picked up the bin beside her desk and emptied the contents into a black rubbish bag.

'Yes, much better, thanks.' She was a bit hungover, but the day felt normal enough. Best to say nothing. She'd imagined it, of course she had. It looked like one thing, but it wasn't. She'd been mistaken. The pen she held dropped onto the floor and rolled under her desk. She got off her chair and crawled into the opening below the desk, aware that he'd have a clear view of her arse. She tried not to care.

'Hope I didn't scare you,' he said.

She frowned, backing out. Often Neve didn't realise he was in the room, and suddenly, there he was. He blended into everything.

'I'm fine, Rob.' She just needed to do what was in front of her. Her desk was piled high with workbooks, and she had numerous emails, including two from her mother asking why she wasn't picking up the landline or her mobile. Beyond her desk was a window that looked out to the built-up seating area, where the year ten girls hung out at interval and lunch. Sometimes she would look out and find Rob sitting out there, his back to the classroom window.

Neve could have sworn she'd been getting a vibe from him at work last term – from the way he spoke to her and shared details about his life while he emptied the bins after school or mopped the floor with a bleach solution so strong it made her eyes water.

'I always enjoy a few wines at the weekend, Neve. I figure, if I'm running most days after work, I can afford to. It's all about enjoyment, right?'

In general Neve talked very little about herself at work, preferring to keep her personal life private. Around Rob though, she almost turned into a blabbermouth, telling him the intimate details of her life. He asked her a lot of questions, maybe that was it.

'Got a man in your life, Neve?'

'I have, as a matter of fact, Rob, a lovely one. Elias. We just bought a brand new bed from Ikea. First new bed I've ever owned.'

'Plenty of time for all that, Neve.'

She got that a lot. She was a young thirty-nine, often mistaken for a student, although recently she'd spotted a few greys. She wanted a baby by her fortieth birthday.

'I'm not that young.'

She hadn't realised how few friends she had in London until things turned bad with Elias. She found herself confessing things to Rob, which she regretted now.

'He wants to see other people.' She had terrible luck with men.

Rob wanted all the details. What exactly did Elias say? How did she feel about open relationships? Had he been unfaithful already?

'Forget about him,' he said. 'He doesn't deserve you, Neve.' He bent over to unplug the floor polisher. 'Breakups are never fun.'

Neve tried to sort through her thoughts. 'I found him fascinating at the start, but actually he's kind of an arsehole.'

'In my experience, someone always wants it slightly more,' Rob said.

Rob wasn't someone whose style would, under normal circumstances, have grabbed her attention, but she was drawn to him. He was at least forty, but boyish, with floppy brown hair falling over one eye. This impression was supported by the black jeans and faded T-shirts he wore, with some band name or another displayed in gothic letters across the front. He was cute, though twice she'd seen him in a T-shirt that said *I'm Sexy and I Mow It*. Rob was the first person Neve had felt an attraction to since she and Elias split up.

'You must miss home, don't you?'

At first, she'd imagined she'd be back in the southern hemisphere within a year, two at the most, either on holiday or for good. But then Covid happened and somehow or other she wasn't.

'Watch the floor there, Neve. Bit slippery.'

'Sometimes. My nieces are growing so fast.' Her family were disappointed she hadn't been able to go for Christmas again. They just needed to know she was all right. Rob retracted the cord on the machine and stood admiring the shine coming off the floor.

'Only took two years of requests.' He meant the polisher.

He pulled a wallet out of his back pocket and opened it, showing her a photo of Zita's kid. Zita was his ex.

'Isn't she a heartbreaker?'

It wasn't a word she'd have used. The little girl had Zita's eyes. Apart from Zita, he never mentioned partners, leaving Neve free to fantasise. He was becoming her new hope.

'Sometimes I try to imagine what a child of mine would look like.' He laughed, puffing out his chest. 'I'd make a good dad, don't you think?'

All those rumours hadn't started from nothing. It was Neve who'd approached Rob as he was leaving the staff party at the end of last term. She'd drunk enough to do it. She'd kissed him in the alleyway outside the restaurant without asking if he minded and put her number in his phone. Partly Neve did it because of the email. It was a few weeks before that she was checking Elias's phone for the Netflix password when it popped up: *Would love to hook up again if you can. I'm sorry for all you've been through. Sounds tough.*

She vaguely remembered Rob going quiet after the kiss.

'I think we better not, Neve. I think we should stop.'

'I just want a fuck, Rob, that's all.' Her hands were up around his neck. 'You can always stop then if you don't like it.'

He was talking. She needed to understand, it wasn't like that. The restaurant door opened, but by then Neve had dropped her hands. Later she couldn't remember exactly who was in the alley before she left. She thought she remembered the empty wine bottle in her hand. Maybe it wasn't as secret as she thought. In the morning there were flecks of vomit in the bathroom sink, and a text from him saying he hoped she got home safely. She tried telling herself that she'd imagined everything, or that nobody knew, that they'd all forget by the time term started again.

A week after Neve kissed Rob, he texted again, asking her out for a drink. It was still the holidays, and she said yes. It was a good chance to apologise, in person. Unstructured time wasn't good. She stayed in her pyjamas and binge watched

Gilmore Girls. She was drinking a couple of bottles of wine a day at that point. Elias still hadn't found a new flat.

'What's taking you so long? You must think I'm a fucking idiot,' she said. She was standing unsteadily in the doorway to the living room. She could have worded it better. She'd been dismantling their bed all day – drinking. She'd dragged it down to the basement. It was the only way she'd get him to budge. She'd thrown a cushion at him. Maybe it was when Elias laughed and slouched back onto the sofa that she got confused. Did she really want to break up with him? His long, crossed legs, two-day-old stubble on his face, the way she liked it. She'd thought she wanted to be light and free.

'You've got too much time on your hands. Talk tomorrow,' he said. 'When you're sober.'

'Hopefully not.' Who was she kidding? He was an arsehole.

Neve spent the week imagining Rob running, wondering exactly how many glasses of wine he allowed himself in the weekend, picturing his flat.

She ordered a glass of wine while she waited. When she saw him walking down the length of the bar towards her, she pretended to check her phone. He was in a button-down shirt and jeans, and he looked good. Lots of women on the school staff fancied Rob, no one bothered to pretend they didn't. He didn't know she was watching him. His eyes slid over the women sitting at the bar. She only knew a few things about him. One of the teaching assistants, Mrs Palmer – Kaye – had said since his divorce he was making up for his lost youth. She said it like it mattered, like it was a thing.

She made her apologies for the drunken kiss, and he brushed it off, changing the subject. He ordered a bottle of red, without asking what she was drinking. Two drinks in, he casually – not really, he'd been looking for an opening – mentioned it.

'You see, the thing is, Neve, that while I've been involved a few times with women my age, married to one even, I'm ultimately attracted to the younger ones.'

'Oh, right.' Neve helped herself to a glass of his wine. She didn't know exactly what Rob was referring to when he said younger. Hadn't she told him her age? Did he just mean younger than him?

'Part of the reason things ended with Zita,' he said.

'I assumed you liked me,' Neve said, feeling her face going red. She'd thought it was a date. He should understand that he couldn't let everyone at work think he was one thing and be another. What did he mean by younger ones? She didn't know. All she knew was she needed a distraction from the situation with Elias, and she liked Rob.

'Oh, Neve,' he'd said, amusement in his voice. 'I do really like you. It's not the most straightforward situation, but I think we can make it work.' He reached across the table and grabbed her hands. 'I'd just appreciate it if we could keep it professional at work, if you don't mind.' That was how he'd explained it. Neither of them said anything for a moment while she thought about whether she did mind, and what he was asking. It crossed her mind to ask what it was worth.

'I guess it makes sense,' Neve said. She thought about him watching the girls at lunchtime. This was only a harmless flirtation, she told herself.

'I do really like you, Neve,' Rob said. He said her name a lot.

'Oh,' she said. 'I understand.' Of course, she needn't take him up on it. 'To be honest, I'm not looking for anything serious right now . . .'

'Now, Neves, don't run away on me again.' He'd never called her that before. 'At least let me take you out for a meal next time?'

She tried to come up with a response, gathering her things. He walked over and put his arms around her, pressing her face into his shirt. She was aware of his soapy, boyish smell, and the pressure of his fingers on her back. She lifted her face and decided that if he kissed her now, she would kiss him back. But before that could happen, he pulled away.

Neve woke up, realised it was Monday. It was the first day of term. She thought about calling in sick. She scrolled through her texts from Rob. *R U up for it? Have you had one? How much have you had to drink mon amour?* Strings of kisses to follow each one.

Lunch? She stared at her phone and tried to figure out why Elias was texting her. Although Neve's feelings towards Elias changed by the hour, she had drunk an unusual amount of alcohol over the weekend and she was hungover, possibly still a bit drunk. And she'd run out of coffee. She hated herself but she texted him back. *Name the time and place.* She could hear him moving around downstairs. Yesterday, while he was out, she let herself in. He'd turned part of the basement into a home office. She took a tube of moisturiser, a scarf, a book left by one of the younger women he was fucking.

'Good morning, Holy Innocents, how may I help?' Rob was always the first person to get to work.

'Hi Rob, it's Neve. Listen, I'm not well.' It was easier to tell a lie than to tell the truth, although she needed to remember the lies she'd told so she didn't repeat the lie too often. She hoped Prue, the principal, wouldn't ask for a doctor's note. If she was a better person, she wouldn't say the thing she said next.

'Stomach bug, had a dodgy takeaway last night, Rob.'

She was too hungover to remember to use her phone voice. 'Could you let Prue know I won't be in today?'

That was the hard bit of the conversation, right there.

There was a long pause.

She couldn't blame him; he wasn't paid enough for this. He was probably just trying to be professional, but at this moment it felt like something else. Judgement.

'No problem, Neve. Take care now.' *Mind your own business*. But somehow her business was his business now.

An hour later, she was buying coffee and a bottle of wine at the Brixton Hill corner shop when work called. The man behind the counter coughed at the exact same moment that Neve picked up and Prue said, 'Where are you?' like she knew what was up. Work was a thirty-five-minute commute away in Tower Hamlets. She looked at the clock over the counter. There was time. She was in a pair of track pants and her running shoes, and it was a chilly autumn morning. Neve ran to the train station and made it to work just on the second bell.

Through the net curtains in Prue's office, wet leaves made a thick blanket on the ground. Neve pictured herself sliding in amongst them till they stuck to her body, like a damp flannel, soothing her head.

'Want to tell me what's going on, Neve?' Neve looked down at her running shoes. Had Rob said something to Prue?

'Sorry?' She wanted to explain, but she couldn't tell Prue about her blackouts. Her voice seemed to be coming from far away. She could hear her own breathing. 'I'll try to do better.' She wanted to feel those cool leaves against her eyelids.

'I can't afford to cover you.' Prue shook her head back

and forth for emphasis and her newly cut hair moved freely. 'The girls need continuity. The parents have started to ask questions. We need you here. Every day.'

Prue was judging her. She needed reliable staff and Neve was unreliable. Rob must have thrown her under the bus. Out the window the spindly branches of the tree waved. There was something comforting about it. Neve imagined waving back but kept her hands in her lap. 'Yes. Sorry.'

A group of year twelves walked past talking loudly, library books in hand. Neve's homegroup would be waiting. She'd assumed Rob had her back. Did he even fancy her?

'Three Monday absences last term, Neve. Three.'

'The students seem to like me.' The girls had warmed to her right away. They'd treated her a bit like a celebrity when she started, hanging around the classroom before school. Rob's comment about being attracted to younger ones formed in her mind as a half-thought, a possibility.

Prue was looking at something now, rustling papers around on the table. 'It's not a popularity contest, Neve. We're paying you to do a job. I met with the board yesterday.' She slid the paper over the table to Neve. 'This is a formal warning.'

Neve's mouth started to twist, to do something she hadn't given it permission to do. She took the paper and sat up straighter in her chair. It seemed right. Prue kept talking. There were plenty of other people in line for her job if she didn't want it. Prue had enjoyed saying that. But after that she couldn't concentrate, not really. She kept thinking about what would happen if she lost her job. Rent couldn't wait, and her credit card was at max. An apricot-coloured gerbera was wilting on the windowsill. Neve folded and unfolded the piece of paper. Prue looked at her. 'Are you sure you're up to coming to camp next week?'

'Oh. Yes. All good,' Neve said. She looked around the room like she was trying to figure it out. She was half in, at most. Nobody could fully commit to orienteering and sharing a room.

'Everything organised for Jenna Brome? We've never allowed her to go before.'

'It absolutely will be.' When Neve asked Jenna if she wanted to go to camp, she said yes with a smile that changed her face completely.

'But can we rely on you, Neve?'

'Yes.' Neve brought herself up to look at Prue directly, meeting her eyes. Nothing could help her. 'Definitely,' she said. There wasn't any way around it. Unless she could think of a thing she'd forgotten about that she needed to do. Prue stood up then and just like that it was settled.

Outside the classroom there was a queue of girls waiting, and the smell of cigarettes. Neve unlocked the door and went in first.

'We thought you might be away again, Miss,' Jenna said. 'Running late?' It was hard to say exactly how the girls seemed different, taller perhaps, more self-assured than before the holidays.

'I had a meeting with Ms Johnson, actually Jenna.' She waited for them to seat themselves and unpack their bags, trying to think of anything except that meeting. She handed out the homegroup photos taken last term.

'I like the picture, Miss,' Sabine called out. 'You look nice.' Sabine was skinny and tough. She had to be joking. Neve's hair was greasy, and she had a huge smile on her face, like the smile was a joke. The joke was on her now, wearing sweatpants at work.

She did the register, while the girls finished off their homework. Rob texted *R U ok?* She checked Facebook and Instagram, turned her phone to silent. There were so many hours left. Better to think about Elias, about the mess her life was in, and how she could change it. She was running out of time to have a baby. She kept her phone out, waiting for Elias's reply, but there wasn't one. Why ask her to lunch, then not answer? Maybe that text wasn't even intended for her.

Caitlin walked into the classroom, looking a bit worse for wear, and wearing a non-regulation sweatshirt.

Neve went up the back stairs into the staffroom, hoping to avoid Rob. It was crowded and noisy and all the chairs were used up. She was hungry, that was it. She ate a piece of toast and then made a cup of instant coffee and stood against the wall, not drinking it. She looked around the room. Everyone seemed fresh from their holidays, wearing new clothes and sporting new haircuts and spray tans. There was talk about local real estate, businesses that were closing, minor tensions at home. Rob was the last one in, and he went and refilled the kettle. She'd hardly said a word to him since their date, except on the phone this morning. Their relationship felt like it had shifted slightly – less flirtatious, although they'd agreed to keep it out of work. There was a pile of pastries on the table. She was about to go and get one when Kaye came over. Kaye always smelled like cigarettes and hair spray.

Kaye said, 'Go away anywhere nice on your break, Neve?' This made her think of her mother who couldn't understand why Neve didn't just jump on a plane to Paris or Barcelona when the fares were so cheap. And when it was right there. Covid was right there, too. The Rona, as the girls called it. The death toll was rising.

'Oh, I gardened and read books,' she said. She wasn't sure why she lied so often. She didn't really mean to lie. What she meant was to not complicate things.

'Any good books?'

'Actually, they were back issues of *Vogue*.' She knew how it must sound. Honestly, the only thing she'd read was a text from her brother saying he knew Neve was having a crisis, but could she please stop causing their mother one. She composed a long text back, but she'd run out of credit.

Prue cleared her throat. She'd had her hair, which was not entirely black and not entirely grey, cut and styled. It was less helmet-like and made her face look softer. 'As you all know, camp at Fairplay House is next week.'

'Nice to see you here, Neve. Looking forward to camp?' It was Lisette, the other year ten English teacher. Neve didn't like her, as a rule, and it was mutual.

'Oh,' said Neve, like she hadn't thought about it, even though it was her who'd organised for Jenna Brome to go. Jenna was excluded from so much already. As if her epilepsy wasn't enough for her to contend with.

Lisette walked over and took a doughnut off the plate on the table. 'I see Caitlin's tablet hasn't come back.' She took a bite. A blob of custard from the pastry stayed on her top lip. 'And no regulation jumper.'

Neve ignored her, and she said it again, slower. Neve tried to relax. Lisette was only trying to look out for Caitlin. Wasn't she?

Kaye leaned in. 'How's Rob?'

It was Kaye's way to ask personal questions in public. Neve shifted her eyes but not her head.

'Um . . . I don't really know.'

Everyone was so convinced they were having an affair.

He was well out of earshot, engrossed in conversation with Shahena, a pretty student teacher. Neve put her at nineteen, early twenties at the most. Before their conversation in the pub, this would have seemed harmless enough, but now Neve wasn't sure. She was scared to be right.

'I'm not sure I'm really his type, Kaye.'

Kaye glanced at Rob, then at Neve, putting them together in her mind. Nobody had owned up to starting the rumour about them, though Neve suspected it was Lisette.

'Look, nothing happened,' Neve said. She was sick of reminding them. And the way Lisette talked about Rob was the same way she probably talked about Neve behind her back. Neve might have something over Rob, now. She could always tell Kaye later what he'd said about younger women, and that would be that. Kaye couldn't keep her mouth shut.

Neve took her coffee into the kitchen. She tipped it down the sink and opened the dishwasher. As she bent over to put her coffee mug in, his hand slowly brushed the length of her back.

'Sorry about this morning, Nevey,' he said.

'We need to talk,' she said. Her head was full of cliches.

When she straightened up, he was standing right behind her and for a moment he leaned into her.

She went grocery shopping after work and bought a bottle of vodka. She would have a little drink today, just to take the pressure off and start again tomorrow. She drank as she cooked dinner. She hated the taste of vodka, but it was the quickest way to take the edge off. After dinner she'd pack for camp. She couldn't stop thinking about Rob. Maybe he was using her. Elias didn't need to be perfect. He just had to be a good father. If he was, he could fuck as many other women as he liked. She sat on the sofa and ate dinner. She kept drinking. She felt the back of the sofa behind her. She needed it there. It was holding her up. She closed her eyes and focused on a mental picture of a body beside her, a body that was both Rob and Jenna but not Jenna. It was a vague shape at first that slowly gained definition – torso, arms, neck. It was more Jenna than Rob. She could hold onto it only briefly before the image dissolved. Three days, she told herself, crunching her fingernails into her palms There wasn't enough time to be scared. She probably should get to bed. She realised that's what she'd been waiting for all day. She was looking for the bit where she could have a drink and feel better and then it would be time to sleep. She would be better. Things would work out – with Rob and Prue, all of them, Jenna, the girls.

Neve saw Jenna first, because she was wearing an oversized neon green Nike shirt. All the girls were standing in front of the school. To look professional, Neve had accidentally over-aged herself, in a cardigan and magenta blouse which might have been why nobody noticed her arrival. When Jenna eventually saw Neve, she waved, and Prue turned around. Prue looked pointedly at her watch and then at Neve. She was carrying a clipboard and wearing a hi-vis vest.

'Sorry,' she said. She had her excuse prepared. 'My train was late.' She was here now, wasn't she? She stood next to Jenna and her mother, in front of the Mother of Mary statue. Parents were saying hello and goodbye. Caitlin's mum and her fiancé were arguing about something. The fiancé was everything, according to Caitlin, that her dad wasn't. Prue and the bus driver stood talking. Neve didn't see Rob until he was standing beside her. He'd had his hair cut and was carrying a duffle bag.

'How are we, ladies,' he said. 'Happy days.'

She reached into her pocket for another mint. She'd ended up staying up too late on Tinder again, arranging a hook-up for Friday. Two could play at that game.

'What are you doing here? You weren't rostered on for camp, were you?'

He rested his bag on the base of the Mary statue. 'I came to see you.'

Neve stared. He did that so well, turned an everyday conversation into flirting. They never really had a normal conversation. How much further was this going to go?

'Too soon?' He laughed. 'It was a joke, Neve. Kaye's broken her ankle. I'm her replacement.' He had an answer for everything. But whatever invisible structure had connected them before, he'd broken.

Jenna's mum looked up from the bench where she was sitting, as if she might say something to stop Jenna going, then changed her mind.

'You must be Jenna's mum,' Neve said, turning her body away from Rob.

'That's right.' The woman didn't introduce herself, just pumped Neve's hand, holding on too long.

'First time away from home for a lot of them,' Rob said. He was trying too hard. For something to do, Neve took her backpack off and unzipped it, then zipped it back up.

'It's a pity your family's so far away, Neve.'

'Really,' she said, more sharply than she'd intended. She'd work it out, take charge of herself.

Somehow Neve ended up sitting across the aisle from Rob, halfway down the bus. It wasn't hard to avoid him at work as he'd wanted, but here they were. She opened her energy drink, looking out the window as the streets blurred past. There was the smell: a heady mix of deodorants and hair products. The camp was nearly two bloody hours away.

Rob kept it light, offered her mandarins from a netting bag. He was trying, she had to give him that. Prue named the towns they passed, the rivers they crossed, and told them what was planted in the fields. Neve went to sleep for a while. By then the land around them was going dark. She drank another energy drink and thought about phoning Elias. He had till the weekend to find somewhere. She could have said any of this to Rob, but she didn't. He knew too much about her already.

The room had bunk beds and the smallest toilet Neve had ever seen. She sat on the bottom bunk. She had started to shake a bit. She wondered what Elias was doing. Probably in their flat, no, her flat, having the best sex of his life or something. Prue's suitcase was against the far wall and an alarm clock and some toiletries were on a table. There was a dressing gown on the back of the door. She was here now, could do it for a bit longer.

The dining hall was loud and brightly lit. At first, she couldn't bring herself to go in. Rob came to the door holding a mug of tea and handed it to her. She drank it fast, and it burned everything in her mouth.

'Thanks.' Her voice gave her away.

'The food looks terrible,' he said, smiling at her. 'We'll get out of here when we can.' It was like he'd read her mind; except she wasn't going anywhere with him.

She went into the kitchen. The caterers had set out trays of lasagne and salads and garlic bread. She counted out Jenna's medication and then re-counted it. Seven tablets, names like Phenobarbital and Tiagabine Hydrochloride.

She checked it with Prue, who gave her a rare smile. *There she is. There's the woman I employed.*

Jenna, Caitlin and Sabine came over, carrying plates on a tray, lasagne squares and different kinds of salad. It might have been the unfamiliar setting, or because the girls weren't wearing their school uniforms, but everyone seemed younger.

'Your birthday tomorrow, Cait,' Jenna said. Neve passed Jenna her medication. So far, the girl was taking everything in her stride.

'How old?' Rob said.

'I'll be fifteen.'

Neve didn't like him knowing that about Caitlin. She wondered what else Caitlin had told him.

'Do you know what you're getting for your birthday?' Jenna asked. Caitlin shrugged, her hair falling forward as she filled a paper cup with juice.

'Do you mind me asking how old *you* are, Rob?' Neve said. She guessed he was about forty. There was an atmosphere between them.

'Oo, lover's tiff,' Sabine said.

'Forty-three.'

Neve tried to work out the numbers in her head but was distracted by Sabine's comment. 'What do you mean, Sabine?' said Neve.

'What do you want for your birthday, Cait?' Rob clearly had no idea about Caitlin's home life. It was a tactless question as *wants* didn't often feature in her family.

'It's Caitlin,' Neve said.

'Oh, nothing Miss,' said Sabine. 'Sorry.'

Neve wondered what for. Such a small moment, surely more imagined than real.

'She means you two are going out,' Jenna said.

It was possible that Neve was losing her mind. It was day one without a drink, and the wheels were already beginning to come off. It was as though her mind was trying to justify something, but it wasn't working, it was just noise.

Caitlin chased the pasta around on her plate, not eating it. 'I'd like to be able to talk on the phone to my dad.' Everyone nodded. There wasn't a lot to say. Her heavily lined eyes welled up.

There was something about the way Rob was looking at Neve. He'd been caught out. He needed Neve to behave in a way that suited him, in a way that preserved people's idea of him.

Neve heard rubber on concrete as people entered the amenities block. She rooted through the wash bag for a flannel. She needed a shower.

She could hear Caitlin and Jenna talking outside the shower cubicles. They were talking about someone Caitlin was considering dating. The problem was that he was boring, as well as old.

'Does it really matter that he's boring?' Jenna said. 'He's kind of hot. And he can pay for stuff.'

Neve smiled at the teenager's priorities. She'd clearly had hers wrong with Elias. Paying for stuff was what was important. She turned the shower on, waited for it to heat up.

'I thought he was younger than forty-three, didn't you?' Caitlin said. 'You know he has a step-daughter?'

Neve pulled the shower curtain across.

'Just before, at dinner, I'm sure he touched me on the back and the shoulder – like stroking,' Caitlin said, giggling. 'Then he stopped.' Caitlin didn't sound like herself.

'I'm confused,' Jenna said.

Something like shame flooded through Neve. She turned the shower off so she could hear clearly. The conversation paused while they brushed their teeth. She braced herself and tried to work out what the help would look like. She felt like she might throw up, but that wouldn't do any good.

'Is he dating Miss, or not?' Jenna said.

Neve heard a toilet flush and a door open.

'He left a note in my bag.'

Neve hated how young Sabine's voice sounded. She grabbed her towel and wrapped it around her body. She'd let them down. Everybody would point to her and ask why she didn't do something to stop this, that the girls deserved better. That was hard to take, but probably it was true. There was no way around this conversation. She came out of the cubicle.

'What did the note say?' Neve said carefully. It was a not-real question.

Everyone seemed to be registering Sabine's words. It wasn't just Neve watching Sabine, they all were. No one wanted to make a scene.

'It said I was a distraction. From his job.' Her cheeks were flushed. Neve looked at Sabine and Sabine looked at Neve and everyone looked the same way. Neve wondered how many times he'd said the same words, and to how many students. There was a lot she could have said, but she was imagining all the ways she might confront him. Sabine opened her mouth like she was about to speak, then didn't. It might involve having to answer more questions. She stared at the ground.

'He wrote his phone number.'

'Will he lose his job, Miss?' Jenna said. Neve thought about quitting her job. She was going over every decision she'd made, every choice she'd got wrong.

'What will happen to Rob?' Caitlin said. 'Did he touch you as well?'

'No,' Sabine said. 'Nothing like that.'

'That's out of our hands, now,' Neve said. 'I'm so sorry that happened to you, Sabine.'

Sabine seemed slightly embarrassed. 'I'll live.' Not really an answer. Now there was no sound at all, except for the girl's slow breathing, reminding Neve to breathe. She was trying to smother the voice in her head shouting that she'd known all along she was right about Rob.

'I didn't call him,' Sabine said. 'It was ages ago.'

The three girls walked back across the grass towards the row of cabins, a few paces apart, their puffer jackets rustling. It felt pointless to speak. Above them, the night sky was thrown with stars, unlike the sky in London. Too much air pollution.

Miss wasn't happy about leaving them but needed the loo. She said she'd meet them at their cabin, three doors down from Ms Johnson's. There was something about the way she was acting – not coping. She told them it was important to pass the information on to Ms Johnson, in case there were others. If there had been a way not to, they probably wouldn't have.

They stood outside Ms Johnson's cabin for a bit, nobody moving. Everything was quiet. They didn't want to get it wrong. Caitlin knocked on the door.

Really it had to be Sabine, because of the note. It wasn't that Caitlin couldn't do it, she needed more time. Everyone liked Rob. But that didn't seem to matter now. What if she'd imagined him touching her? Nobody else had seen it, not even Miss.

'Has something happened, girls?' They'd half expected Ms

Johnson to know why they were there. Now it seemed like a test.

'Yes,' Sabine said. It was a kind of relief. Miss walked across the grass towards them.

'Some things have happened,' Sabine said, holding herself straight. Caitlin and Jenna agreed, with nods. It would be Sabine's fault if he was arrested.

Ms Johnson looked at them with raised eyebrows, like she didn't like the sound of that.

'All right,' she said, her face swinging across to Sabine, then back to Caitlin and Jenna. 'What things?'

Miss was standing outside their cabin, taking everything in. Ms Johnson asked all the same questions that Miss had asked. They tried to answer the questions honestly.

'Well,' Ms Johnson said. 'If you're certain. If you're quite sure.' She was going to need them to go over it again, probably more than once.

For a few seconds, Caitlin was sure the girls' puffer jackets looked brighter, lit up, flashes of colour against the night. But then they got dull again.

Ruin

Grace always sat at the bar at the back of the Cambridge, where she could watch who came in. A huge mirror ran the length of the pub, so you could sometimes watch people without them knowing. The mirror made the place seem a lot bigger than it really was. There were always people she recognised even if she didn't know the names that went with them. Nobody knew her name either, but she'd always get a few nods and that was enough. There were the old men in their corners or at the bar alone, then the younger ones. Sometimes one of them would ask if she was okay and if there was anything he could do for her and she would smile and nod, although she was never sure which question she was responding to. Today was Friday and in an hour or so the place would be rammed. The girl behind the bar noticed her and raised her eyebrows in a friendly way but there was also something else in her look. Grace pulled at the sleeves of Mattie's cashmere cardigan that she'd been wearing everywhere. She still hadn't washed it.

Grace didn't actually know what she would say when Mattie arrived, or how she might begin. Mattie was two years older, and Grace was used to her sister talking first, but she had some questions. She hadn't seen Mattie since they'd flown back from the Gold Coast, was it a month ago? Two? In separate seats. Mattie hadn't even waited for her at the baggage claim. Grace thought she'd spotted her getting into a taxi outside the airport in Wellington, but she couldn't be sure. It had been just a glimpse of red shorts and what looked like Mattie's suitcase.

A man was sitting at the end of the bar. She'd noticed him before, probably because he was the right age. The old ones were usually too deaf or too far gone or both. She couldn't be sure she hadn't talked to this one before, not that it mattered. He wore a suit, and he had that dense stubble that stayed on your face even after shaving. He ordered a drink.

Mattie was late now, as predicted. She always suggested a place in town, nearer her work, but Grace had made up a story so they could meet here. It was here or the flat and the flat was a tip. There was a musty smell in the bedroom, like mouldy fruit. Even with the window open onto the weirdly warm air, it hadn't gone away. Also, people kept coming to the flat. 'How are you?' they asked. 'How are you? Do you need anything?' Asking questions. On and on where there were no answers. And so, she came here, where she didn't know anyone, and the men didn't ask anything of her. That wasn't nothing. Some could even be generous after a few drinks. Work was still paying her but she wasn't sure for how much longer.

She tried not to look at the man sitting along from her but looked anyway. He had taken off his jacket and was scrolling through his phone. His stubble was greying, but his hair was dark. She cleared her throat.

'I'm Grace.'

He flinched slightly but waved.

He introduced himself but she forgot his name straight away. He had long fingers, no wedding ring. She bought them both a drink and moved along and climbed onto the stool next to his. She raised her glass in a toast, and he did the same but didn't clink her glass. Listen, she wanted to say. Listen to me.

It was getting harder to hold onto the facts. Grace was uncertain now if she believed herself or had accidentally made up something that wasn't true. She hadn't seen Mattie for a few weeks before the Gold Coast trip. Maybe that was why she kept swinging back and forth between things that happened before the trip and the events that happened after. She tried to make herself stop thinking about it.

Then she ran into Mattie's colleague Ruth from the radio station at the bus stop. Was it a fortnight ago? Or longer? Grace had gone to the bus stop with the intention of going into work. But she'd ended up just staring into the road.

'How are you?' she'd asked Ruth.

Grace wasn't sure what Mattie might have said to Ruth. How much did Ruth know? Why wouldn't Mattie answer her calls? Mattie and Ruth had worked together for five years; shouldn't Ruth know Mattie well enough by now? If you know someone, you should be able to read the signs, you should be paying attention. Grace had spent years expecting Mattie to understand her. Was she unknowable? Was it her or Mattie?

'All I know is she's super angry at you,' Ruth said. 'She just said you had a fight and you disappeared all night and almost missed your flight.'

'She should at least answer my calls,' Grace said.

'You might want to do something about your drinking,' said Ruth, then got on the bus.

Grace felt like something had been unleashed that she couldn't put back. And it wasn't going away. At first, she wondered why Mattie hadn't talked to her, but then, immediately, she wondered how Mattie could do such a thing.

Mattie had been in one of her moods that night, but she looked beautiful when she came out of the hotel bathroom in a bathrobe, her hair slicked back in a bun, her lips streaked red.

'Gracie!' She held up her hands, palms together. 'Sorry. I'm thinking we should go out, get drunk. Let's pretend to be each other for the night. Here, put this on.'

Mattie's dress was expensive-looking and made from black stretchy material. Grace took it and put it on the bed. She got undressed quickly and pulled it over her head. She tugged at the fabric. It only just covered her arse.

'You're so thin again,' Grace said. She would have killed for Mattie's legs. She hadn't inherited their mother's thighs and Grace hated her for it.

Since the restructure at work, things were different. Grace worked as a host at the big gallery in town. They didn't get to move around much. Sometimes she had to concentrate to stay awake. They were only allowed to sit on a stool after they'd worked four and a half hours of a shift. They could read if things were quiet – not on their phones – but you could read a book. A book was useful but sometimes people wanted to talk about the art. The pay was terrible but there weren't many jobs she could do, and if she was careful, she could cover everything. The gallery provided uniforms, which saved a bit on clothes, usually a T-shirt printed with the artist's name and name of the exhibition. The current one said, 'How does your body feel?' on the front. The slogan had attracted a lot of commentary, from men mostly. One man came in near the end of her shift. He'd walked with purpose, stopping to look at one artwork, before stopping in front of her. He asked what was showing in the upstairs galleries.

'It's install week unfortunately, only this main space is open.'

He slowly read the words on her T-shirt out loud. 'How does your body feel?'

She shifted on the stool. If she was someone else, she would have said, 'Tired, my body feels tired of men like you,' but she didn't say anything.

'I'd like to find out.' His eyes moved across her breasts then up to her face.

'They're for sale in the gift shop.' She let her eyes drop from his and whenever she thought about it now, she realised that by doing this she had shown him the power he had and that he could have done whatever he liked.

Didn't you do anything, Gracie, for God's sake? Fucking predator. It's our responsibility to call it out.

She should have called it out. But she and Mattie were different. Even though they'd come from the same place they were still different. Mattie had a career and was saving for her Forever Home. There were lots of people who'd be happy to take Grace's job. That much was made clear by Carlos, the new director, when she'd got to work late a couple of times. Carlos was from somewhere in Europe.

'Gracie, are you even listening?' Mattie had on a silky maroon item of Grace's, not a dress, or a jumper. It draped off her shoulders and was belted tightly at the waist. 'Let's do this. We'll switch. I'm you, and you're me.'

'Are you sure this dress—' Grace looked down at herself.

'Is hot enough? It's way better on you! That booty, though.' Mattie whistled and laughed, and Grace tried to say something else, but Mattie's laughter took over. This is how it was with Mattie, always being pulled forward, up out of how she was feeling into something else.

It was a good night. The barman emerged from a crowd of people at the bar. Mattie and Grace saw him before he saw them. They saw his skin and hair, eyes and teeth. Something was going on with him – hot. Mattie stood behind her, with hands on her shoulders, a voice in her ear, and Grace could not stop staring at him, and Mattie was laughing and drinking and asking the boring questions that got them talking. Questions like, Where do you live? What do you do for work?

'It's Grace, actually.'

'Whatever you say, *Mattie*.' He'd taken her hand.

She felt like a bad actor. 'Who told you that? Did my sister tell you that?'

'You did. So, what do you *do*, Mattie?'

Grace readied the words in her mouth. 'I work on the radio, mostly.'

His name was Luca, and he was almost finished his shift. She tried to answer his questions in a way she wouldn't normally. Later, when he told her she looked good and he kissed her, she let him.

Mattie, being Grace, held the room. She told the gallery T-shirts story, recalling what Grace had told her, somehow changing it up in her radio voice. Her hair was coming loose from the bun, and she was all bone and skin and laughter.

'So, it turns out he was just a little bit sexist after all.'

Grace got up and leaned over to take the wine bottle from the icebox. She was a bit shaky at hearing Mattie's words and with everyone's faces looking.

'That is a serious piece of arse.' Only Mattie could get away with that.

'Can I've a go of this?' Grace asked no one. She sat back down and peeled off the foil.

'We took him to court and sued the bastard.' Mattie would have, too. She could afford to, but also she would have liked the drama of it. It was hard to know what to think about it. It was hard to make yourself the hero of your stories, but Mattie was. Grace tried to remember that it didn't matter. Because it didn't, not really.

'Of course, not everyone saw it that way.'

'What?' Grace tried to hear the words without feeling them, but in that moment it all seemed more important than any of it really was.

Mattie reached over and patted her arm.

'You remember, Sis, someone was too scared to speak up. In the face of misogyny, someone let the sisterhood down.'

Grace felt her face burn and wanted to explain everything. She could feel Luca and the others listening, enjoying it. She wanted to tell them she'd had a mind to complain but she'd been worried she'd lose her job. That it was easy for Mattie with her perfect legs and her voice and her Forever Home. She didn't have the words for that much. She knew it was a mistake before it came but it came anyway.

'I'm Mattie and I make myself throw up after any food. I'm so desperate to be thin.' Grace pretended to stick her fingers down her throat.

The silence hung between them, and in this moment, Grace became Grace again and Mattie was herself.

'Fuck you, Grace.'

Mattie had closed the door of the Uber at the exact moment Grace stepped forward to get in it. Grace wished she hadn't let the Uber door close. Then they would have been together. The more Grace thought about it, the surer she was. In that glimpse she had of her sister, there had been something, like she'd been wanting a reason to leave.

The trip to the Gold Coast had been Mattie's idea, of course it had. Mattie had all the ideas.

'Come on. It's been forever, Gracie. You can pay me back. It's going to be warm! Do you want me to get depressed this winter and kill myself?'

'All right, yeah, we don't want that.' Grace tried to smile. It was easier to be grateful than to refuse. Mattie did this. Made everything the most dramatic version of itself. You loved that about her, Grace reminded herself.

She didn't actually remember seeing Mattie on the flight back from the Gold Coast. She didn't remember Luca's apartment or how they got there, or when she began to come here to the Cambridge every day or when she grew angry at the men she talked to, or when everything began to remind her of something else. This is what she remembered: Mattie taking off the bathrobe, all ribcage and pelvis in matching underwear. Mattie lazing on the hotel bed, eating sweets and flicking through a magazine. Mattie painting her nails. Mattie who made a better job of everything, Mattie who never seemed to end up in bad situations and didn't have to wear a stupid uniform at work. Why did Grace feel like she was the one in the wrong? She hadn't ruined anything. If anyone should be angry it should be Grace.

Grace looked down at the scratched surface of the bar and she could feel her face flushing, but she kept going. She held tightly on to the whisky glass. The man, whose name she'd forgotten, rested his chin in his hand and his face didn't move. She told the story. How she'd changed her mind about wanting to fuck Luca the barman.

'I don't want to,' she'd said. His friends had come in to watch and when he finished, they'd called out to her and had a turn, and it was too dark to tell their bodies from everything else.

The man looked at his glass the whole time and not at Grace's face. He was hardly there. He hadn't touched his drink, but when she got to that part, he picked it up and drank till it was gone. He said something, but in a voice so low she didn't hear it. She took Mattie's cardigan off and put it over her knees like a rug. Mattie would know what to say.

The man leaned over the bar to get the bargirl's attention. 'Two tequila shots.'

Grace sucked on the lemon, hungry. She looked up at the blackboard at the day's specials. Fuck it, she'd have the steak and chips. She'd been vegetarian for two years but lately she'd been waking up craving meat, imagining blood pooling against the lip of the plate, the taste of metal against her teeth. She worded in her mind the email she would send Mattie. Not tomorrow, but next week, not angry, just disappointed, sad to miss her.

No – she would still come. She'd been held up at work. Mattie would phone and apologise soon, explain everything. Grace pulled her blouse down over the slight bit of flesh visible over the top of her jeans. It seemed to be straining over her chest. How had she not noticed that her jeans had a rip in one thigh? It was like her body was overflowing out of itself, refusing to be contained anymore.

The bar was packed with people now, but the man took their bags to a table nearby and bought them a whisky each and a pint. He loosened his tie and undid the top two buttons on his shirt. He was a bit too quiet. Mattie would have asked him questions: Where do you live? What do you do for work? Want to come home with me? Perhaps Grace had been here longer than she meant.

The man said something and laughed. The music had been turned up and she had to lean in closer to him to hear him as he repeated it. He was drunk. It showed in his face. He laughed again and she laughed but shook her head because she didn't want to have sex with him.

The steak arrived. She cut into it and cut little pieces of meat off, eating until it was gone. She laid her knife and fork down, then mopped up the leftover juice on the plate with the bread roll. She wiped her lips with the back of her hand. The cold fat had left a coating on the roof of her mouth.

He was still talking. 'Tell me the rest of it, then.'

She put her head back, held her hands tightly together. It was almost a relief to hear him asking. This was her story – some lies, some uncertainty, but hers. She tapped her phone, tried to stay present. She called Mattie's number. It went to voicemail, as usual, Mattie's voice teasing as though she was undecided as to whether she would really return your message.

'She'll call me tomorrow.' Wait. That was all Grace had to do. Not go forward or back, just wait. She tried not to reach for the phone again. It had probably been a bad idea to leave the flat today. She was so tired. Oh god, she was tired. 'I'm fine,' she said again. She was always fine right up until she wasn't.

It had been daylight when she found the hotel. Mattie's bed was empty and unmade and an angry note said she'd gone to the airport. Grace took off the dress and tights she'd been wearing, placed them on the bed in the shape of Mattie's sleeping body, like those cut out clothes and paper dolls they'd had when they were kids. She got in the shower and stood under it. The warm water stung. She'd had too much to drink. There was a misunderstanding with Mattie. What a weird night. She should have tried harder to stop it, called it out. She was having trouble remembering but something bad had happened, the way they sometimes did to people. There was no point reporting it, not in that dress she'd been wearing. Mattie's dress. Why had Mattie left when she was needed the most? She must have her reasons. Was Grace the reason? Why wasn't she here? Grace needed to figure it out. And get to the airport.

A Safe Place

Vivienne scrapes her blonde hair into a high ponytail before inspecting her face in the mirror. Her skin looks parched, and the whites of her eyes are streaked with red. First, she rubs moisturiser in, then smears foundation into her forehead and cheeks. Next, concealer over her spots, pressed in with her forefinger. Her eyedrops spill over her lower lashes. She applies two coats of mascara. It's like she's colouring herself in. Her eyes almost look rested now. On the dresser is a photo of her on her wedding day, with her mum.

Every morning, Vivienne cycles with her daughters to school. It's a good ten minutes, mostly downhill. Yesterday, a woman in a SUV pulled up at an intersection where they had stopped and rolled down her window.

'I hope he gets a life sentence,' she shouted.

Did she not care that Ines and Ellie were in earshot? Vivienne mouthed fuck you, and they rode on. Before, Vivienne was a contained person. But now there was nowhere for her to contain anything because nothing was private anymore.

Vivienne's friend Sadie said, 'Stay home for a while, people will come around', but Vivienne wouldn't give in. They'd done nothing wrong.

Six weeks ago, two police officers came to arrest Giles, her husband, for downloading images of children. Giles kept saying 'I'm not a paedophile', but they took him into custody and removed all the computers from the home, including Vivienne's personal laptop. They would do a deep scan.

The mist has come right in off the harbour and is settling into the far pockets of the garden. She can just make out the playhouse. She puts her slippers on and goes into Ellie's bedroom. Ellie has turned her bed into a fort, using a chair and some rugs. Her rag doll Trixie is on the floor – so well-loved she has lost an eye.

Giles was questioned for twelve hours, then eventually they ushered Vivienne into a horrible concrete room. And they said, 'Giles has got something to tell you.' That's when he confessed, if you could call it that.

He said, 'I've seen some things.'

Across the hall from Ellie's room is a smaller room, with a desk and a leather armchair, one of the ones that swivels. Vivienne doesn't go in there, not anymore. That's where he sat to download and look at the images. After dinner most nights, with a glass of Jameson's.

'No, you haven't just *seen* things,' she'd said. 'You went *looking*.' Her anger had gotten the better of her. This was what happened, wasn't it? He'd gone looking for it.

There's a screen between me and them. It's a virtual world.

How had he even started going to chat rooms? Her niece, Tara, second year at university, was now boarding in that room because, as Vivienne rather bluntly told the girls, it wasn't as though their father was going to be moving back in. There was a futon wedged beside the desk now. She could understand him becoming addicted to a thing, but it was very hard to understand him becoming addicted to that.

Ines had the room down the hall. She never picked up her clothes. The weekend laundry was always Giles's job. At fourteen, Ines was worryingly childlike but had recently started using Vivienne's eyeliner and become concerned about gaining weight. Ines was fair haired like Vivienne, but, as Giles had often noted, very much his child around the eyes. Not anymore.

Recently, Ines had been using the trauma caused by her father's sex offending to get out of doing things.

'I'm fine. Just leave me alone.'

While it hurt that Ines wouldn't confide in her, Vivienne was worried she would become one of those rich kids with no focus. Vivienne had promised she could continue to see her father – she was connected to Giles in a way that Vivienne wasn't, in a way Vivienne couldn't explain other than by blood. Vivienne wouldn't even have a photo of him in the house.

Vivienne stands at the sink, rinsing plates, putting them into the dishwasher. Dinner crumbs on the table, Ines's plate untouched. She pictures Giles sitting across from her, clean shaven, working on his laptop. They'd enjoyed a glass of wine after work, talking about things that mattered, or didn't. A past life.

Their marriage had been in trouble before, after Ines was born. Vivienne ignored it for a time, and it got better, but then she had Ellie and it got worse. Maybe it was another baby or maybe it was something she did or maybe it was nothing at all. She remembered saying it.

'I'm not happy.'

He hadn't asked her *what* she was unhappy about. She had watched his mouth and his dark eyes. Her mother had often said that Giles had beautiful eyes. Wasted on a man, she'd said. After that, everything had built and built and then spilled over. But of all the things in the world that were her fault, this didn't seem to be one of them.

Giles was released on bail, and they'd driven home. A week later he packed and moved out – 170 kilometres away, to a caravan on his cousin's farmland. Before he left, she pushed for details, asking about the ages of the children.

'I can handle it,' she said.

He said he'd seen pretty much everything. Which came as something she couldn't comprehend, really. As far as she knew, they were a happy, ordinary couple. What was wrong with her? Just stick with what was right, what he should have been looking at, which was her.

She turns the dishwasher on and goes down the hall to check on the girls. It's important there are no gaps for thinking or spare moments for thoughts to slip in. But the thoughts come anyway, ramming into one another before she can ward them off. And then they are there whether she likes it or not. She's always known how to get on with things, how to keep busy. But she doesn't know how to get on with this. He's ruined us, Vivienne thinks. Shouldn't Tara be back by now? She was a grown woman – but Vivienne can't help feeling responsible, with her under their roof. She'll call Tara and she'll answer. Things will be fine.

Lynne, her sister-in-law, called her as soon as they heard.

'I'm so sorry,' she said.

Family came before everything. All those horror stories of being disbelieved by their families: that wasn't happening to her. I thought you blamed me, Vivienne didn't say. She asked about them, their trip to Rarotonga. The food so fresh, Lynne said, sunsets like you've never seen. This wasn't why she called. She wanted to know why Giles did what he did. As if Vivienne should know! Vivienne wished she could tell her, beyond the obvious: he didn't even like sex that much with *me*. She wasn't sure where to begin. Maybe Lynne could help by telling her what it was they already knew?

Thinking too much muddied the waters. Last year, Vivienne ran a half marathon with Sadie and a few others from the neighbourhood. Or was it two years ago? She remembered she pumped and dumped, so Ellie was being weaned. They'd taken over Sadie's bathroom the evening after the race, drinking wine while they did their hair and make-up. Intoxicated with the lack of responsibility. At the party, Iain from number thirty-seven tried to engage her in a conversation about the ecological damage they were doing to the world. Iain was Ines' friend Sage's dad. Vivienne wasn't interested in why she'd done it. It might have been sleep deprivation. Or the feeling that if she didn't make something happen, nothing would happen. It was an unremarkable fuck. Giles had always occupied the prime position in her life.

'David and I were talking,' Lynne went on. 'You don't think he ever . . . nothing inappropriate with the girls, do you, Vivi?'

What had been a flicker became something more steady. Vivienne saw the girls and Giles bouncing on the trampoline: piling up on the mat, laughing.

'We don't think Giles is a terrible person, do you? Just somebody in pain with nowhere to place it,' Lynne says.

Vivienne replayed the trampoline pile up in her head, concentrating on where he put his hands, but it was impossible to tell what was memory and what her mind was making up.

'Listen, it's Ellie's bath time, I'll have to go. Lovely to hear from you.' *Bath time*. Vivienne hadn't really been thinking of *speaking* those words. Often, she thought about what the most wrong thing to say or do would be, in any situation. Yes, she owes them a visit. She must do that soon.

The news had spread fast. It was the kind of neighbourhood that got together for Guy Fawkes and held a sausage sizzle for the children. And Halloween was an event that even Vivienne and Giles looked forward to. Most of the street refused to speak to them anymore. Some neighbours were better at hiding their disgust than others, but it was still hard to go walking. Some people had a way of not looking. Did they hold her responsible in some way? Did they see her as immoral, by way of association? She started going running after dark, leaving Ines to read bedtime stories to Ellie.

Vivienne steps outside, lighting a cigarette. The second time today, although it's getting late. She tries to go outside at least twice a day. Otherwise, she feels trapped.

It was Giles's idea to move here, near the best schools. She was just getting used to it when all this happened. Before, she wouldn't have called herself naive. She knew about the world, her head was on straight. But now her voice locked in her throat when she thought about what other people might know, that they might be repulsed by the sight of her. Her good and quiet husband. It was a terrible version of himself, he'd said. Like he'd told himself a story so that it became something he could live with. And Vivienne had laughed and said, You have no idea. She didn't want a part, or the children to be any part, of it. They'd get bullied. She pictured it – striding across the school playground, grabbing the kid and shaking the hell out of him. Ines was only fourteen and Vivienne could see her struggle to make sense of it all. It was impossible to explain it, but the reasons for her dad leaving were important to Ines, so they had to try.

Vivienne stayed away from the trial, but it made headlines. Deviant sexual interests, the judge concluded, before reading out the sentence. Giles's career was finished. Nothing was found on his work computer, nothing they could pin on him anyway. You had to wonder, all-girls high school, his preferred demographic. Chocolates at the end of term, thank you cards. Overworked, stressed, and perhaps that had led him to make bad decisions that had adversely affected the people around them. Sorry girls, your father has failed you.

Vivienne flashes the headlights. As soon as Ines is inside the car, Vivienne feels lighter. All morning, she swum in their pool and worked on a story for the magazine she edited. Ellie was at day care.

Ines does up the seatbelt, across the beginning of boobs and Vivienne starts the car. She was, overall, fine with the arrangement, which was that once a month, Ines would meet her father here, at this always busy café.

'He cries every time,' Ines says as she gets in the car.

Probably fake tears, Vivienne thinks.

'Starting over has been hard on his own. I hope he meets someone soon.' Ines scrolls through her phone.

'Do you think that's realistic, after what he's done?' Vivienne asks, pulling out into the traffic. 'Surely he'd have to tell that person.'

Ines has developed this irritating habit of asking questions and then getting bored halfway through, asking another one, and then giving up. She'd been talking about her father's sex crimes a lot recently. She'd mentioned it at the mall and heads had turned. Vivienne asked quietly that she lay off, but Ines had waved her mother's protest away.

'You're in denial, aren't you?' Ines had said, louder still,

'You'd rather not face up to this stuff.'

Vivienne had walked into a store, away from her. She wished she'd been able to protect the girls. Gossip got around fast.

They are halfway home, Ines still scrolling on her phone. 'Hon, it's hardly my stuff to face up to, quite honestly.' Somehow, Ines seems to hold her mother responsible for what had happened.

'Well, everyone has a past, Mum,' Ines says. 'He'd just have to meet someone who could understand that there's more to him than his crime.'

'Very few people would, Ines . . .' Vivienne brakes to make sure she is only five kilometres over the speed limit.

'Just because you're uncomfortable . . . makes you think that other people would be equally as uncomfortable.'

'Sweetheart, he wasn't just looking at naked ladies.' The car stalls a few times up the hill, but Vivienne eases it along, making a mental note to book it in for a service.

'Yeah, I just think it's more complicated than that – he was unhappy. And not thinking.'

'Perhaps you don't quite understand the idea of . . . taking responsibility?' Vivienne says. 'For your own actions. I mean we are in control of what we do.'

'You don't really understand depression. I can join the dots, which make a lot of sense to me . . .' Ines trails off.

'What do you mean, join the dots?'

Ines stares out the window and doesn't say anything.

'What, you can sort of imagine how that would happen?'

'I can see how it might happen.'

'You sound very . . . forgiving, Ines. You know, it's different for me – you're flesh and blood. It's a different . . . betrayal, really.'

'Depression isn't logical. It's just a collection of atoms and it's possible to change your thought patterns. You shouldn't blame someone for being depressed.'

'There's nothing wrong with being depressed, you're missing the point.' An urgency has crept into Vivienne's voice. 'Isn't it about values? Doesn't it reveal something about your father's character?' Vivienne knows she is on the cusp of saying all the wrong things so doesn't particularly mind when Ines interrupts.

'You could start by asking some questions.'

Vivienne grips the wheel. She doesn't need Ines to tell her that. If Giles was here. But he wasn't. He'd caused this bloody mess.

The road is narrow now, full of sharp turns and hills. The Pacific stretches out below them. How good it would be to be floating in it, weightless and unafraid. She has no real memory of the drive from the cafe.

'Sweetheart, I don't think you comprehend the weight of bringing you and Ellie into the world.' While a part of her knows she drove safely, she can't recall intersections or lane changes, or how long they waited at such and such. The conversation was unnerving.

'There you go again,' Ines says.

'I know I'm always saying it, and you get tired of me saying it.' Home is three streets away.

'Go ahead, Mum – ask the question of the day, everyone else is.'

'Oh, all right. Fine.' Giles always knew what should be done and how. Fuck Giles. 'There are some things I can't articulate because of what they might mean.'

'That makes no sense.'

Vivienne opens her mouth, but no words come out. Neither

of them speaks. When they pull into their driveway, Vivienne feels like the world has ended around them, but they don't know because they are inside the car. It isn't a safe place.

'I can't bear the thought of anyone hurting you.' There, she'd said it. She owed her daughters that much.

'You're kidding, right?' Ines laughed. 'Oh. You're not kidding.'

Ines told her mother that recently her routine had been wake up, throw up, go to school, come home, throw up, sleep.

Vivienne leaned across and put her arms around Ines, and her shoulders tensed, but she put her head on Vivienne's chest. The luck of it. It was a safe place, after all.

Vivienne goes to Sadie's, and they sit by the pool, drinking beer while they watch the kids swim. Vivienne is still uneasy in public – the school gate, the coffee circuit.

'Does anyone even speak to him?' Sadie asks. 'Monster,' she says, under her breath. She takes a swig of beer.

'Can we not talk about him?' Vivienne says.

They talk instead about Tinder.

'Are you sure you're ready?' Sadie says.

The frequency of sex had diminished when they became parents, but she and Giles had a lot of sex in the early days. It was high quality. Nothing outrageous – Giles had seemed straight up – but he knew what she liked and how to get her there. He was sexually confident, and this appealed to Vivienne. There were no doubts.

'What can I say?' Vivienne says, scrunching her hair on one side. 'I know what I want.'

'I think you've changed,' Sadie says.

Vivienne looks at her friend. She promised Ines she

wouldn't tell Sadie. She wants to tell her yes, she's changed. Everything has changed. Ines is at home watching TV and probably eating ice cream to throw up later, and Vivienne is struggling to think of a time happier than this. They could talk to someone about that. They were intact.

The following week, Vivienne requests the police file. She needs to try and understand what has happened to their lives. Maybe by seeing it on a page, she can restore a kind of order in her mind. Join the dots, or so she hopes. But here is the thing – without this report in front of her, she might doubt that any of it occurred. There are aspects of it that she thinks she might even have made up. The best she can do is be there when the girls need her.

Doctor Ink

By the time Sinead found out Joe was married to Kaylie and they owned the print studio, the sex was already there, or it wasn't there yet but it was arriving. Something about the secrecy had excited them in a good way, not a secret exactly but not discussed. Sinead had taken a beginner's class with Joe. There was something about him. Those deep-set eyes and long eyelashes. She'd booked private instruction to perfect her lithography technique, and he'd offered her a job. The studio was called Doctor Ink and ran workshops and held events, as well as printing T-shirt and tote bags for businesses. Sometimes art students used the space and there was always music. It felt like an exciting place to work.

She looked at her phone. She was lying in bed, in the exact spot the printing press used to be, recalling Joe washing down screens wearing latex gloves. The cracked leatherette seats had stuck to her thighs. She could still see the indentations in the floor left by the wash troughs. At the end of the room, the doors opened into what had been the washout room. Joe's mountain bike was propped up against the wall. This made her remember the finances again and she opened the banking app. She transferred the amount for the new gallery into Joe's account, more than she'd had in her entire life, and waited for the payment to be confirmed.

The house was so quiet, she would just stay here. It wasn't like her to lie in; there were so many jobs, but she wasn't used to the lack of interruptions, or the absence of noise. She'd been so tired lately, fainted at work – low on iron. It had been quite nice, disappearing for a little while.

Afterwards, Joe had suggested they go out for a steak, even though she was vegetarian. He was always joking around, so different from Sinead's other boyfriends. She'd always gone for men who took themselves too seriously.

Joe had left to pick up the glass for the new gallery window before she was awake, and the house was cold when she eventually got up. Moving into the print studio was her idea. It made sense. She'd sold her house, and they were using the money to set up next door to the old studio, just an espresso machine and a gallery space with a limited number of prints. Joe had called it a fresh start and Sinead agreed, without saying out loud that it was more than that, it was her investment, her chance to make something of this. It was what it represented: the thing she had worked so hard to hold onto. The new place would be in Sinead's name. She needed to show the community and Kaylie that she'd won. This was a small town. They needed to stick it out. The long tables and stools from the print studio had all been sold now, and the little stage where Kaylie once stood for the screen-printing demonstrations dismantled. In its place, a heap of dirty washing in the wicker basket. It looked like someone else's life, not hers. At first, it had felt strange to be away from home, like she was avoiding something. She would need to go back to her own life now and then, to do her washing, dye her hair, feed the cat.

'We'll be a blended family,' she'd told her two. Veronika had shrugged and carried on swiping through her phone. Nat had grabbed her skateboard and gone to the skatepark without saying a thing. Joe's kid, Knox, just carried on, as though Sinead didn't exist. But he had been angry a lot last summer. Joe was training new staff and Kaylie wasn't coping so Knox went to stay with Kaylie's parents, Barb and Alan. It was hard to know what to think about it. Or feel about it. Sinead had written a few emails to Kaylie but hadn't sent them. They'd all have to adjust; she was putting herself first this time. She hadn't, since Dave, her ex, left. He had been fucking his assistant. The shame Sinead felt hadn't come from the affair, more from all the time that she'd wasted. Nat wasn't even a year old when it happened.

She walked down the hallway picking up items: two jumpers, a sock, a homework folder. One end of the upstairs was Veronika's room now and Knox was at the other. Nat was in the old toilet block next to her and Joe's room. It needed windows. The new toilet was under the stairs. She looked in the hall mirror at herself – her makeup was smudged around her eyes. The robe was loosely belted, one breast partially exposed. Now, when making decisions about what to wear, she thought of Kaylie. More eyeliner. Redder lipstick. Dangly earrings all the time. Kaylie made her look bad, so she would look like Kaylie. She straightened the hall runner with her foot. The plain ones were nicer, but the patterned ones were on special. They'd painted the hallway a shade of grey that she'd chosen only after trying out twenty other colours, but the place still retained its smell of emulsion and lacquer. What are you doing? the building seemed to say, probably echoing most of the bloody community.

Downstairs, there was a huge hole where the drying racks had been, and a refurbished barn door was going in. The bin in the corner was jammed full and there was a trail of last week's dal spilling onto the floor. There were papers strewn across the table, and she looked at the printed letters, which talked about money and demands. She put on a coffee. It was the stovetop so it would take a while. It was good to take things slowly.

Joe got home well after dark that night. From the sofa, Sinead watched him pacing on the deck. He was wearing his boxer shorts and an old Doctor Ink T-shirt. Merchandise sales had gone up after the Kaylie incident. That was the kind of community it was. Nothing ever happened, so when it did, everyone wanted a part of it. Joe was on his phone – to who this late? She turned the volume down on the TV.

It was Barb and it was something about Kaylie. Joe spoke slowly, telling his mother-in-law things she wanted to hear, consolations. I'm sorry, it will be all right. Yes, she was still his mother-in-law. The kids were fine. No, they hadn't noticed any changes in Kaylie before she went away. Was it wrong to say they hadn't noticed? That they were absorbed in themselves? The sliding door banged. Joe threw his phone on the coffee table and sat down on the sofa next to Sinead.

He talked relentlessly, throwing out statements and bits of information, stressed, talking over Sinead when she tried to reply. She gathered Kaylie had taken her clothes off in Arrivals at Auckland Airport. She was coming back from India where she'd been discovering herself – her words. Security put her in handcuffs and flew her down to Ward 21.

'Fuck, okay, she's not dead.' He ran his fingers through his hair. 'Christ, sometimes I think she just does it for attention. She's been a bit out of sorts since the change . . . in our living arrangements.'

'Can we just—' she said.

'Of course. It's just a bit of a shock. I'm still processing it.'

'What do you mean, out of sorts?' Sinead shook her head,

moving away from him on the sofa. She was visualising Kaylie taking her clothes off. Last year, Joe didn't ever mention Kaylie's lunacy towards Sinead to Barb and Alan. Why hadn't he brought them up to speed? Sinead hardly recognised her own voice when she said, 'I hope you asked how we can help.'

'Yeah, sorry,' Joe said. 'Nothing compared to last year.'

Sinead remembered the broken crockery, Kaylie's injured hands, her embarrassment afterwards.

'She just told me she skipped her meds a couple of times,' Joe said. 'Barb said she was withdrawn the night she stayed with them in Auckland. Her and Alan won't be down for another week.'

Sinead looked at his bare feet, tanned against the pale concrete floor, and noticed his hairy toes. She didn't remember his toes had hair.

'I take it you haven't told Barb we've moved in together. Does she even know Doctor Ink has closed?'

Joe didn't say anything.

'You haven't told her.' If it was a question before, it wasn't now. Sinead didn't know how much Barb and Alan knew or what to say about Kaylie.

She stopped for a pack of cigarettes at the kiosk at the entrance to the hospital, before carrying on down the glass corridor that linked the buildings. Her footsteps somehow sounded like an intrusion. Outside, the rain was practically horizontal. Hardly anything was allowed in, and most items had to be left at the front desk, like the raspberry muffin she brought from home last time she visited Kaylie.

'I'm here to see Kaylie Manning.' She put as much normality into the sentence as possible, putting the cigarettes down on the counter.

'Hold on one moment.' The receptionist pushed a buzzer on the wall. 'Take a seat.'

Kaylie was sitting on a chair, leaning on the wall. Her black hair looked unwashed and was coming loose, wet circles formed under the arms of her grey pyjamas. Sinead stood there for a while then moved over to the other chair, pulled it closer to Kaylie's and sat down. Kaylie didn't move or look at Sinead, her heavy-lidded eyes and thick brows completely still. There was no sound at all, except for her slow breathing. It was a bit much; she wasn't a statue. Sinead wanted to kneel down and shake her awake, help her to stand. Perhaps if she did, Kaylie would revert to her old self and speak clearly, they could have a conversation. Sinead lifted her hand, paused. Kaylie's blue eyes were looking right at her. Why did she? Why did they? It hadn't happened all at once. It would be easy to say they saw it coming. This was what they'd tell people and probably people were being told that. Probably, Kaylie hadn't been well for years and this could have been foreseen.

There were no surfaces at the studio she and Joe hadn't been familiar with, the wooden tables, the printing press, the toilet cubicles. That night they were upstairs in the office. It was late, about two in the morning. Joe was sucking on her nipples and she'd just pushed him down. She watched his head working over her vulva, looking for her clit and then he had it – she'd always imagined they'd just get caught. When Kaylie appeared in the doorway, unable not to see, their clothes strewn around nothing to do with her, the orgasm was too good. A noise came from the back of Sinead's throat that she didn't hold back.

It wasn't their finest hour. Or was it? Weren't they exactly where they wanted to be? Either way, now Kaylie had evidence.

The next night, she'd told the entire workshop Sinead was stealing her life.

The planning of it all, the timing was so Kaylie. Later, Sinead imagined her looking up the roster – how to manage it, what time to make the announcement – the effort it would have taken. Sinead had never asked Joe to leave Kaylie and the kids or to be with her and they'd never spent the whole night together, just fucked. It was as though once Joe left Kaylie, they no longer shared a frame of reference. But Kaylie was here now, in front of Sinead in the middle of the psych ward, just to reassure Sinead, if she needed any reassurance, that Kaylie was, and probably always had been, unwell.

A nurse came into the room with the medication. Her lipstick was a garish pink, and some had smeared on her teeth. She put the plastic cup down on the bedside table.

'Why don't we get you dressed? You could take your friend outside and get some fresh air.'

'People round here don't like being told the truth,' Kaylie said.

What had Sinead expected? That it'd be different this time? She wanted to fill the gap, but nothing came, so she held up the cigarettes. Kaylie brightened so instantly Sinead almost laughed.

'That's why they all gossip. The nurses say there's no hive mind but it's not true.' Kaylie's face was doing so much. The nurse helped her off the chair and began taking off her pyjama top. Sinead looked away. Talking would mean they'd have to discuss it and they'd never talked about this thing that had happened. She could say, 'I'm sorry for what we did to you, Kaylie.' She wasn't sure she meant it, but she could say it.

'Look, there are a lot of stories in here,' Kaylie said. 'So I don't need to make anything up. They'll tell you they're good stories, but they're not true. So, let's stick to the truth, me and you.'

Outside, the rain had stopped. Kaylie was even thinner than before. She still had that slow confident walk, long strides, swinging her arms apart from the walk, nothing about her felt familiar.

'Stop following me around,' growled Kaylie. 'I don't need to explain myself to you.'

Everything was wet in the large, circular courtyard. The walls were high, and silvery-grey ivy was creeping up the bricks.

'Shall we sit?' Sinead motioned towards the only dry seats under the awning.

'That's not necessary.'

Sinead took out one of the cigarettes and lit it, imagining Joe's hands on Kaylie's waist, her breasts, her hair. She passed the cigarette to Kaylie, who accepted it, making a sound like a piece of food was caught in her throat. Her hair was sticking to her neck. Kaylie hadn't smoked before Joe left her, and now she did, yet somehow the most normal thing about her was the smoking. Sinead wrapped her denim jacket around herself and folded her arms. Visiting hours were between 10.00 a.m. and noon. She wasn't sure how long it'd been.

'Do you need anything?' Sinead asked.

Slowly, Kaylie smiled. She came forward now, closer to Sinead, too close, her face against Sinead's. Each time Sinead moved away, not directly back, but a tiny step to the right, Kaylie matched her movements, so they moved in a circle as she spoke.

'I know what you're up to,' Kaylie said. 'Everyone knows.'

She nodded her head, so the cigarette in her mouth bobbed up and down.

'I've got an idea,' Sinead said. 'Let's not talk.'

Her phone rang. She reached for it, but Kaylie grabbed her shoulder. 'Careful,' she said, 'careful.' Kaylie giggled, laughed. 'You got what you wanted. You wanted and you wanted. Fuck. Fuck no. Is it Freya now, or Rhiannon? The dark-haired one?'

Kaylie asked for Joe, where he was, when he was coming. Then she would think he was there, talking to him. Sinead stalled her. He was busy at work, he was coming. The questions came at her, and she tried to answer.

'It's getting to you,' Kaylie said. And then she started talking about something else.

It had been busy in the studio, constantly. Joe arranged caterers for the big events, and they worked out of the tiny upstairs kitchen. The hens' party workshops were always well-attended. That night was Eve Taylor's and Kaylie was Eve's maid of honour. It was a hot night. Sinead was working with another group in the upstairs studio because Rhiannon had called in sick. The workshop smelled of rosemary, red wine and printing ink. The hens had created a makeshift dance floor by pushing the benches back after the T-shirt printing workshop. The music, which seemed louder than usual, had stopped. Joe was demonstrating how to make a stencil with a latecomer, and Sinead was coming downstairs with more squeegees. Kaylie was standing on the stairs, glass of wine in one hand. 'Excuse me.' It was rowdy and no one took much notice. Right then, Sinead knew what it meant. She didn't know how Kaylie would play it.

'Sorry to interrupt!' Kaylie shouted, and gradually the

talking lessened, then stopped. She stepped around Sinead and positioned herself at the front. She was drunk, nobody could argue with that, but sober enough to know what she was doing.

'Kaylie,' Sinead said quietly. 'Don't do this.' There was a heaviness inside Sinead's body, like a weight going down into water. She glanced at Joe for help, trying to meet his eye but he'd removed himself to the side of the room and was watching Kaylie. She dared him in her mind to look up, go on, go on, come closer.

'Everybody knows Sinead, one of our finest staff members here at Doctor Ink.' Kaylie paused. 'How long have you been with us?' She was asking Sinead, or anyone.

'I haven't really thought about it,' said Sinead, smiling hard at Kaylie.

'What are you asking that for?' Eve shouted.

'Two whole years!' Kaylie said with a slow wave of her hand. Then, 'Can you believe it, Sinead!' She found Sinead's hand and her grip tightened over it and Sinead thought *she is stronger than me*. There were a few claps, and someone said, 'Speech, speech!' Joe's eyes bounced from Kaylie to Sinead now, then back to Kaylie.

'You've achieved so much, in such a short time.' Kaylie turned and touched Sinead's hair with her free hand before Sinead could move, making her hair fall across her face. Was this the end? Maybe this was the humiliation that would end it all. But that wasn't important now; what mattered was the impulse, the way she reacted and what she reached for – tune it out, she'd done it before. She felt the strong, cold pull of the river, moving past her, towing her away. She had occasionally wondered if she was too old for the backless dresses but had worn them anyway. It wasn't a crime to want to look nice. Go ahead, Kaylie. She pictured Kaylie, lying at the bottom of the stairs, her dark hair covering her face.

'*This bitch* is fucking my husband. She's trying to *steal* my *life.*'

'Well, clearly fucking you is such a non-event.' Sinead almost laughed when she said it. She wanted to shake Kaylie, but she just said, 'You might need to take some responsibility for yourself, Kaylie,' and tried to find a way to move down the stairs. For someone so small, Kaylie took up a lot of room. Sinead couldn't stay where she was, but she couldn't get past.

'You're dreaming if you think that fucking other peoples' husbands will get you to the top. You're having a fucking laugh.'

'Are you finished?' Sinead asked Kaylie. 'Tables five and nine are waiting on squeegees. Oh, and find someone else's fucking hand to hold.' She pulled her hand out of Kaylie's and looked around the room, which suddenly seemed alive, made of soft moving skin and hair. Her eyes began to blur. Kaylie was crying now, although it didn't stop her from talking. She'd been talking for a while, getting whiny. With all the light and the sound Sinead didn't hear any more of what she said, she just smiled and smiled.

It was a Sunday at the studio, a few weeks after the hen party. Sinead had been on all day with Freya, who was working a double and Rhiannon had just arrived for the evening workshop. Sinead and Freya drank coffee and talked about the Kaylie situation while Rhiannon washed screens. Sinead's daughter Veronika was helping her.

'Why do you still even work here?' Veronika asked. 'It's not like it's well paid.' Veronika had always known everything about the situation, probably more than she should.

'I know.' Sinead looked at Freya. Everyone knew how much she was doing. 'I do actually like my job.' She could work school hours or weekends when the kids were at their dad's. When they were little, it had seemed like she might never work again. She liked being there before they opened, ironing T-shirts, making the gallery look nice. It felt as though the completion of these simple tasks were the first steps to living the life she deserved. 'The pay isn't that bad – and it's going up soon.'

Rhiannon laughed. 'Okay Sinead,' she said, feigning a business tone. 'You organise that.'

Sinead listed more things then, named them, because she'd lied – the pay was barely enough to support her and the kids – although then it began to seem pointless again, to her and Veronika and maybe to the others too. She didn't know. For a while it seemed like she could maintain it. The job couldn't last forever. She should ask for more, more, but she was biding her time. This was just the start. You couldn't rush Joe.

'I'll talk to Joe,' Sinead said. 'I'll ask for more money.'

Rhiannon snorted with delight. 'Yeah, okay, talk to Joe. Cause Joe has a handle on the money.'

'It's complicated.' That's what Sinead said to anyone who asked, but Rhiannon wasn't asking. Everyone knew Kaylie did all the accounts for the business. Rhiannon laughed again but didn't say anything else except 'talk to Joe' under her breath, which started her laughing again.

Sinead went upstairs to the office. The weekly roster had to be written up, and the T-shirt order put through. She hated this small town, everyone claiming a monopoly on everyone's personal business. Rhiannon wasn't everyone, but still. She went into the office. Joe was on the phone. She squeezed into his side with a quick hug. Sinead was sure it was Kaylie on the phone. Sometimes even the thought of her – her name was unbearable again – would untether something in Sinead. She thought about her a lot – like all the time. He'd rearranged the roster so Kaylie and Sinead never worked the same shift, and in that moment it had seemed enough. Except it meant she was paid for fewer hours. And Kaylie was another woman who knew her boyfriend as well as she did, who saw him on the days she didn't. She constantly thought about them together at work, holding staff meetings and having lunches, the times he'd had to stay over because Kaylie needed help with Knox.

'Why won't you leave it alone?' Joe was saying. 'You know what happened. You know what the story is.'

Something was about to happen, or maybe it had already happened. Sinead mouthed *roster* at him. He wasn't getting anything done, with that going on. He passed her a piece of paper, with something typed on it. Lists reassured her, made her feel things were in order.

'No. Look, I have to go.' He hung up.

'I don't know why you bother answering your phone,' Sinead said.

'I can hardly just ignore her, Sinead.' He sighed. 'We have a kid together, in case you'd forgotten.'

'What did she want this time?"

'We were talking about Knox, actually, about limiting his screen time.'

There was silence, except for the music from the studio – someone was singing along.

Joe reached for Sinead's hand across the desk. 'You're obsessing over her, so it seems worse than it really is.'

'Because every time we're together it's like she's here with us.

She's here now. Can't you feel her?' Sinead gestured with her hands. She wished they were fighting about something else.

The hard thing, as Sinead saw it, was that something had happened, and it was private and then it wasn't. And now when people thought of her, Sinead knew, they didn't really think of her. They thought about Kaylie and Joe and the things that Sinead had done.

'I've been hearing how much fun she is at work. Without me there? Is that what Rhiannon meant?'

'Oh, come on babe, it's not like that.' Joe shook his head.

'Not like what? Apparently, everyone would rather socialise.'

'Rhi talks shit with everyone. I know what you talk about when I'm not around.'

'Even if we did talk about you, how would you know?' she asked Joe. He wasn't the only one with allies. 'Are you still fucking her?' It sometimes worried her; the way Joe could suddenly look like a place she'd never been. Nothing happened, he always informed her, after any shifts with Kaylie. It was as though he didn't know if he was lying.

'You know she told Rhiannon she'd decided not to look for another job? Apparently, I should be the one to go.'

'She's always been crazy, Sinead. How can you believe anything she says?'

Sinead wondered just what Kaylie said, how she might have put it.

'These look good.' She meant the latest tote bags, piled up on the desk. She chose to stop the thoughts, stop the voices, though maybe not all at once, maybe turning down the volume just so she knew she was the one in control, reducing the noise.

She heard him turning around, ready to say something

like 'You look good' in a kind of sexy joke way but she wasn't there. She was already walking out of the office.

Sinead's studio key went missing, there was a hole cut in her new jacket. She wasn't paid, or she was underpaid. Sinead started taking records of everything, writing events down. The first time her car was egged outside her house she cried to Joe about it. The second time she just hosed it off and drove away.

'Oh, I could tell you some things,' Sinead said to Rhiannon and Freya. They were preparing screens for the evening workshop. Afternoon sunlight was hitting the wooden front verandah and their shadows were intertwined on the studio floor.

'Like what?' Rhiannon asked. She was pretty, brown eyes, piercings up and down the ridge of her ear, in her early thirties at the most. Joe only employed young people because he didn't have to pay them as much. Sinead wasn't sure it was right. Some of them didn't look that much older than Veronika.

'The real reason Kaylie hates me.' Gossip worked both ways. Freya leaned in, sipping her coffee. 'She can't handle the fact that I wasn't interested in her.'

'No way,' said Rhiannon.

'She propositioned me one night when I first started here. Then a week later, I was cleaning the loos and she just appeared in the doorway. She just stood there, watching me clean. I didn't know what she wanted at first, so I asked her, but she didn't answer me. When I tried to go past, she pushed herself up against me at the basin.'

'That's awful,' Rhiannon said. 'What'd you do?'

'What could I do? Since then, she's been making shit up

and telling everyone I'm a homewrecker.'

'Does Joe know?' said Freya. 'Did you file a complaint?'

'I wrote it down, so it's on record,' said Sinead.

'Of course, if it's men, if it's women—' Freya made a sweeping movement with one hand.

'It's still assault,' Rhiannon said.

'I'd like you to keep quiet about this,' Sinead said. 'I mean, don't tell anyone. Not even Joe.' Even as she thought about it now, she was distracted by the idea that Kaylie could have come onto her in this way. She imagined it. It would have begun with Kaylie instigating. They were in the work toilets. Sinead was washing her hands, her shaggy fringe getting in her eyes. Kaylie came out of a cubicle. She said nothing, not even hello and walked over and pushed her body against Sinead's, so Sinead's back was pushing hard into the sink. She brought her hand gently to Sinead's face, kissed her, briefly, then for longer. She stroked Sinead's clit through her clothes. The answer was yes, but Sinead didn't speak or move.

Freya's phone vibrated inside her bag, and she bent down to get it out. It was the next day and they were at the studio again.

'I still can't believe what happened to you,' Rhiannon whispered, watching Sinead closely.

'Long black, cheers Rhi, you lucky fucker on coffees today,' Freya said. 'My neck is literally killing me after yesterday.'

They laughed at this – Freya said *literally* about everything – they always laughed.

Joe laughed too but he didn't say anything, just crossed the room and stood behind her. He started massaging Freya's shoulders. They were all there, Sinead and Rhiannon and the other staff, but even though Rhiannon laughed, afterwards she looked over at Sinead, eyes wide, mouthing *what the fuck?* Freya didn't even say anything, she was looking at her phone. She laughed, maybe that was why he kept doing it. He just did it to wind her up. He did this thing with his knuckles and Freya made a sound, too small for the others to hear, but in bed that night he told Sinead he heard.

'You're terrible.' She'd punched his arm. 'Did you even wait, give Freya a chance to say no? You treat people like entertainment,' she said. 'You joke and you prod just to see which way they'll jump and how far. She didn't want a massage.'

'Like fuck she didn't.'

Freya had told Sinead she had promised herself this was the year she'd have sex again and Sinead had told Joe. Did he want to fuck her?

When they had first compared their sexual histories, Joe had told Sinead he'd slept with around twenty women, and she'd told him her too, and he'd made a joke about having a threesome one day. She often thought about that moment and wondered why she lied.

Freya was attractive and they'd probably both thought about it. They didn't talk much about that stuff anymore. They always had to work and there wasn't time to talk. At work he always had a comeback, a joke, a pickup line that cracked people up, that she fell for every time. He was like this with everyone, had names for all the waitresses. Rhiannon was Blender and Freya was Feisty. 'They'll kill you if they hear,' she said to Joe. 'What?' he said. 'It's a compliment.' She had no idea how he did it, how he got away with the things he did.

Sinead kept visiting Kaylie. The thing she liked was that sometimes she could touch her now, hug her, hold her hand, cut her hair. She cut them short matching fringes. Joe and Knox came on other days. Sometimes, when Sinead arrived, Kaylie would turn away, demonstrating she wanted to be left alone, other times she had plenty to say, talking about things that didn't matter to either of them. Sinead got used to how she rambled on, and something kept her coming back. You couldn't take anything too seriously in here and it was good to be away from the house. The house was still filled with everything that went on. Kaylie chain smoked, couldn't quite look at her.

That day, she thought Kaylie wasn't going to say anything but then she said, 'People might want the truth, but then they won't know what to do with it.' She addressed these remarks to the plastic hospital bracelet on her left arm, pulling at it as she spoke. 'It's all under control, you're a cool customer. We'll see how cool you are when the truth comes out.' It wouldn't have mattered if Sinead hadn't been there at all, this wasn't a conversation, more something Kaylie didn't want to keep to herself, as though Sinead knew exactly what she was talking about. How much did Kaylie know? Nobody understood Kaylie like Sinead did. She was playing a game with herself, in denial. Maybe she should tell a lie, like they wanted. Now she'd told them that Kaylie was in love with her. She could shut them up by saying that Kaylie had been severely depressed for years. She could say anything. Maybe she would.

'Did you know I was there that night? When I came to the studio and found you fucking Joe?' This was what Kaylie did to you, when you thought you had a grip on things, everything shifted around her like a wound. Sinead couldn't recall talking about Joe. There was something she wasn't saying. But it wanted to escape, like a secret that was too big to keep. 'Was that part of your plan, Sinead?'

'I don't know what you're talking about,' Sinead said.

They'd listened – for the first time – to the new Beyoncè album, borrowed from Rhiannon. He talked as though it was laid out – he'd move out, it'd be sweet, Kaylie would be sad, they'd move on. Sinead knew it would never be that simple.

Joe got up halfway through the album, to go to the loo. Sinead waited a moment, then stood up and walked over to his jacket, hanging on the back of a chair. She'd reached into the pocket for his phone and opened it and texted Kaylie. *We've hurt each other, babe. Working late, come over?* When Joe came back out, she was getting undressed.

She'd seen Kaylie in the doorway seconds before she pushed Joe's head down. Looking back, she saw she tricked herself into believing she wasn't responsible for Kaylie finding out. She had wanted to tell someone, but also to keep it to herself forever. Right now, she could see who she was, and what she looked like. She could see what Kaylie saw. The life she'd worked so hard to rebuild. All the work she'd done to reinvent herself. If anything had been laid out before, it wasn't anymore. She was tired and she hadn't eaten. It was as though everything was falling away. Her phone buzzed in her hand. There were two texts from Joe, in reverse order: *I'll take that as a No then.* And the first, letting her know he and Knox were having dinner with Barb. *Want to join?*

'Can I have a cigarette?'

She lit a cigarette, handed it to Kaylie. She lit one for herself, tilted her head in Kaylie's direction, straining to make out what she was saying.

'Is he sleeping with someone else, do you think?' Kaylie looked at her now.

Sinead shrugged. 'Probably. Definitely.'

She was a maker, she wanted something solid to show for

it all. Now she could see this too – that all the solid things she enlisted would weigh her down. Time changed everything. Eventually these things would get further away and then nobody would talk about them anymore. Wait, she thought, wait it out. She didn't feel like going home that night. Her kids were with Dave, Knox was at Barb's. When she stopped, she felt almost ashamed. It was like the shape of Joe moved through everything, eclipsing Kaylie, even her. Kaylie could be Freya or Rhiannon, or Veronika. She could be Barb, or Sinead. Why had none of this occurred to her?

'I texted you that night, Kaylie.' When she said Kaylie's name, Kaylie said it back, like an echo. 'I got you to come to the print studio.' She reached for Kaylie's hand.

'You set me up,' Kaylie said.

Sinead nodded. She couldn't deny it. It occurred to her then that Kaylie probably knew her better than anyone. She half wished Kaylie would make a scene, do something. But she didn't. Wasn't Kaylie angry with her? She knew every awful thing Sinead had done. But it was more than that. It actually mattered to her; Kaylie mattered. Kaylie was a part of her.

'I know,' Kaylie said, like she had read Sinead's mind.

Kaylie stuck her lip out, as though she might cry, but then she didn't. It was like she was trying to decide.

Missing

Naomi looked around the room. The Calmbirth Educator stopped talking and looked at them and smiled. Six other couples were already sitting in a circle on bean bags. Naomi looked at her partner, Pete, who met her eye. He was always so calm, just doing what was in front of him. She wished she was home on the sofa looking at Instagram.

'Kia ora koutou.' Pete lifted his eyebrows towards the group. Naomi sat on a beanbag and tried to get comfortable. When she got pregnant, she made him sign up to beginners te reo at the Wānanga, something she regretted. She had dropped level four after three sessions.

'There's just so much going on right now,' Naomi had said. 'Is there not enough going on?' It sounded defensive in her own ears. She wished they could microchip people with te reo. The only chip she carried was one of shame because she couldn't speak it.

'Do you want to learn?' he'd asked. 'Won't you find the time, if you really want to?'

She needed that chip, so it could protect her from the shame; that shame slid into everything.

She was hot. She took off her sweatshirt. Her body had changed so much that nothing fitted properly. Everyone else seemed comfortable. The Calmbirth Educator was wearing a purple tracksuit and had a high ponytail.

'I struggled to find people in the UK wanting to embrace

this philosophy, so we moved here,' she said. 'The movement was founded first in Australia.'

This was the furthest Naomi had ever made it into pregnancy, but this didn't seem the place to say she didn't know if there would be a baby. At thirty-eight, it was a geriatric pregnancy, and sitting here, with her back aching and her hair streaked with grey, she couldn't deny it. Her hands squeezed tightly into themselves. There was the abortion, ten years ago, after someone used her body without permission. Her sister recently got pregnant by accident, for the second time. Lately she'd been trying to think of the baby as a silent friend, going with her to the supermarket or the library.

The Educator smiled at Naomi. Even the scrunchy in her hair was purple. 'We'd love to hear from you. This is a safe space.' Naomi wasn't in a position to argue. She and this mother of four, birthed in a yurt, might be inhabiting the same space but it didn't make it safe. Just then, the baby kicked.

'Kia ora. I'm Naomi. Twenty-eight weeks.' She'd been trying to keep track but wasn't sure of the accuracy. 'My midwife said this might help with my anxiety.'

'Our emotions have the power to have positive effects on our birthing experience. It's about harnessing that anxiety and transforming it.'

The Educator kept talking. She'd been talking for a while. It was possible to visualise the length of labour they wanted and make it a reality.

'You realise how stupid that sounds?' Naomi whispered to Pete. 'So, if I visualise a one-hour labour, can I have one?'

'I visualised eight hours each time,' the Educator said. 'Gave my husband time to fill up the birth pool.' Everyone except Naomi laughed. 'I saw a tunnel of white light with my daughter.'

The light wasn't white. There was grief stored up in Naomi, grief that didn't even belong to her and it was cordoned off.

They meditated to the voice of an Australian man who said they could be whatever they wanted, just as long as they wanted it enough. Naomi tried hard not to, but she doubted it. It didn't ring true. It was like when people talked about equal opportunities.

At lunchtime, there were fruit platters and hummus and cucumber sticks. Everyone got a tote bag. Afterwards, Naomi and Pete walked across the road to the Settlers Museum. It was undergoing reconstruction.

'Local Māori welcomed the first ship carrying British settlers here in 1840,' Pete read.

'With open arms,' Naomi said, making a face.

'I can just picture you standing on the beach doing a karanga for me,' he laughed. His parents were ten-pound poms, something she'd only vaguely heard of before she met him. When they first got together, he'd impressed her with his extensive knowledge of the land wars. But lately the jokes felt old. It felt like mansplaining. She lifted her face to the sea breeze. The water became almost unswimmable because of the discharge from the abattoir after the settlers arrived. It was a popular swimming beach now, but Naomi never put her head under.

The afternoon session was all about oxytocin. The Educator said slow dancing would get the oxytocin flowing. Pete put his hands on Naomi's hips and pulled her close. He was looking at her in a way that seemed to shift the molecules in the air.

'Ātaahua,' he said, in her ear.

She pulled his ear lobe. 'Taringa.' They started laughing like they might never stop.

Recently, he stuck little white word labels on objects around the house; paraihe niho toothbrush, rorohiko computer, rūma room. He almost spoke her language better than she did. For some reason, no matter how hard she tried, or how many wānanga she sat through, the words wouldn't stick. She had the wrong ears to learn languages, anyway.

It was early morning and the pain doubled her up on the bed and made her grit her teeth. Naomi tried to remember a meditation from the course. The one with the body as a landscape. She was pretty sure she was doing it wrong and then another contraction came, and she couldn't remember anything. Pete was looking around. Checking they had everything.

They had everything.

'You want to call Christine?'

Naomi shook her head. Christine wasn't back from Queenstown till tomorrow. They could phone the back-up, but it'd be hours yet. Pete put on the podcast from the course. She told Pete to turn it off. Pete talked to her mum, but Naomi couldn't hear what they were saying.

The hospital was too warm, but everything looked gleaming and cool, all the shades of blue. There was this smell, like something plastic in the walls and floor and furniture. Naomi had to concentrate in a way she'd never had to before. Pete timed the contractions. Later, Pete said she had this look, like she was fighting something he couldn't see.

Then pale bodies and faces pressed in, the sound of shoes on Lino and a room of people she was supposed to trust. She could hear someone wailing, a deep building wail, like kuia do. She tried to listen deep inside, fixated on the glass pane in the door, imagining it breaking, the fractures splintering outwards across the glass like cracked ice. Her body made a traitor of her and broke, whipping its head back and growling, exposing teeth and hair to the ceiling. When the baby finally came, it came with fists raised, into the scrubbed clean arms of others. There was no noise for far too long and then there were the littlest sounds of life. Someone said, 'It's a boy.' She heard Pete giving the karakia. After that, all she could hear was crying.

She lay beside the baby, looking at the dark shock of hair that had surprised her. Her eyes would not close. She forgot exactly who broke the news about their whenua. At first, she hadn't understood. The hospital was full, and the ward was busy. Nobody had looked at the birth plan or the other form, and nobody remembered Pete reminding them.

'It wasn't worth keeping. It was a bit of a car crash, actually.' As though it was her body's fault. Or a thing no one wanted anymore. Naomi imagined the pēpi and the whenua entangled, her huge floppy belly encasing its deep indigo spread. Touching its collapsing centre, its ridges and lines, the borders bumping against her skin.

Someone had taken their whenua and incinerated it with the medical waste. She imagined the flames spreading and burning, scarlet darkening the steel. Naomi's own whenua was buried at the house on Smith Street in Ōtākou. Now she remembered her mother telling her when her brother was born the nurses had already thrown out his. Naomi imagined anger being passed through the wombs of her tīpuna to her mother who passed it to her.

She must have drifted off. When she woke, the pain was everywhere, and the cot was empty. She went out into the hallway and looked through the tinted glass into the nurses' station. A blonde nurse was holding her baby while another nurse looked at the ID bracelet on his arm.

'There's no name. Shall we write his name on it?'

'No, no. Definitely not.'

Christine had looked at the birth plan, covered in Naomi's writing. 'You can't have tea lights in the hospital. But we'll sort you out a lamp or something.' She wrote something on the paper. 'What's this? Whenua?'

'Yes. I've ticked the box to say we want it kept,' Naomi said. 'My aunty made a . . . vessel for it to go in, in her ceramics class.'

'Right. Might pay to remind them nearer the time.'

And they had reminded them, hadn't they? Where was the ipu whenua Aunty Steph had made?

On the third night Naomi finally did sleep and had a dream in which she went down to the Dirty Utility room and searched through yellow bags. Her whenua was in the Kopa Paru room. All the bits fitted together like a puzzle but there was no way of knowing if the puzzle belonged to her. She picked things up, one by one then dropped them again. When she woke up, crying, and scared, Pete was standing at the end of the bed, saying something to the doctor.

It was drizzling and the air smelled different. Pete put the capsule with Bubba in it in the back of the station wagon, checking everything twice. Naomi reached down and pressed her hands into the damp earth. The lock on the driver's door was still busted and Pete climbed in the passenger side. The rain had flattened his hair.

Naomi got in the back with the baby. The woollen hat had slipped down over its eyes, and she readjusted it. Her body was sore and leaking and her belly looked strange, like a half-deflated balloon. She wondered what would happen to her insides now. She pictured the whenua shrivelling up and rolling out of her in bits, rotting and dark like old fruit.

What day was it? Wednesday? Maybe Wednesday. And it was January.

The car pulled away from the hospital and she thought of her mum and how she took all three of them to their marae after the divorce, how she had never taken them before, when they were younger, and she wondered if her dad was the reason. The weather thudded against the window and the glass shuddered. The rain fell hard, making it difficult to see anything clearly.

Naomi made the baby a nappy, putting kawakawa balm on his bum. She was getting good at nappies. They still didn't have a name.

'What about Dylan?' Pete said. He'd never have suggested that once.

'I don't want any old name,' she said, pressing her hand to her chest. 'I want something that belongs to me.'

Something about them had changed, and she'd gone to a place that Pete couldn't follow. She threw the dirty cloth in the bucket, which was almost full. Things would feel better if she could get her head down, but this baby was unrelenting in his dismissal of sleep.

On Christine's last visit she weighed the baby. 'Hungry boy! You'll blink and this guy will be walking. Any name yet?'

Naomi shook her head. A government letter had arrived yesterday about this, but she hid it. Time didn't feel fast to her. It felt slow and deliberate, like the drip of the breast pump. She watched the baby every second of every day. Her old life seemed a long way away.

On her way out the midwife left a box of condoms on the table. Naomi shut the front door. Sex was the last thing on her mind. Did everyone want access to her body? She was constantly touched – feeding, holding, clung to, pulled, stroked. She picked Bubba up and sat on the sofa. She wanted a beer, but she hadn't pumped.

Pete put his arm around her and nudged closer. Naomi looked at him in a way she might have to apologise for later. The lounge felt too warm. She put the baby on the floor, and it pedalled its legs like a helpless insect. It was as though it didn't belong inside. She went into the bedroom and hooked up the pump.

Two years passed, slow and fast at the same time. Pete no longer asked about their day and hardly seemed to notice that Bubba was there. She spent the days looking for Duplo and half-chewed crackers. She left food in places she knew he would find it, on top of the toy box, on the windowsill where he had started to climb. He was at that stage where walking was basically just not falling over and he fell over often, impressing her with his drive.

'I keep getting the feeling I've lost something,' she told Pete. 'It's driving me mad.' Objects weren't always where she thought they were, as if everything was just out of the corner of her eye. They opened and closed drawers, pretending to search. She found small dirt offerings in the hallway, and Bubba held his hands out to her, and they were full of mud. Relics came up out of the ground here, bits of glass, old ceramics, bricks, and bones. He took her hand, tugged her along, his little wrists circled in fat. They went out to the river. It wasn't always clear who was leading and who was following. The mud at the edge of the bank was thick. He watched his gumboots sinking in.

They floated, forming islands.

She ran the bath and put him in it. She called him by his name, though it wasn't his name really. There had been a time, early on where they'd tried out a few stupid sounding names for him. He covered his face with his hands. She shifted along the edge, so she was sitting parallel with him. It was somehow harder for them to come together now that he'd grown. She no longer worried about crushing him in her sleep, though the feeling she was harming him, unintentionally, was strong.

She often felt Pete's gaze on her, as though she was a thing he deserved. She pretended not to notice, and instead made a mental list of everything about him that annoyed her, he kept walking in on her in the loo, wearing her favourite sweatshirt, his slowness on fixing the lock on the back gate, despite her reminding him. Illogically, she began to wonder about the parent-child resemblance, certainty, probability. It was important she kept this from Pete. Why had she invented this story? Did she believe it? Was she beginning to believe it? All she really knew was that they couldn't name her son.

She picked up the phone, intending to explain to her family that things were going missing, that she was questioning paternity, that Bubba was still without his rightful name.

She couldn't.

The last time she talked to her mother she'd made things up, assuring her things were going well. It must have been believable because her mother hadn't phoned since. When Naomi finally did call, there was no answer on either of her parents' phones and the texts she sent remained unread.

After a week, she called her largely estranged brother. They'd never been okay. Her bro had punched a hole in the wall during their last fight – a stupid argument about drinking. That was how it went, they fought about something stupid, Naomi said something mean, he lost his temper and broke things until Naomi upped and left. Some things were better left unsaid.

Someone at his flat said they couldn't remember the last time they saw him.

She woke in the night to the absence of Pete, and it was relief she felt, which she took as a sign. Her face felt cracked and dry. She hoped Pete wouldn't come looking for them. The only proof of them would be in the photos he took. Now she could prepare for what came next.

By the river the darkness was beginning to fade. The bank was uneven, pitted with holes. She dug for a long time, and it was tiring work. Bubba scooped up earth, then watched it dampen around his feet. The ground had been loosened by the rain, opening in front of them, and Naomi threw the mud to either side, making a kind of trench. The river sloshed forward. She saw her hands against the ground in the faint light and the skin was the same dark as the mud. Bubba poked a stick into the mud, as if searching for something. Then he dropped the stick, stretching his arms and his hands towards her.

From a distance it could have looked like a burial or even suicide, but it was neither of those things. Something had happened when their whenua was thrown away. She didn't remember what the first thing to go missing was, but now she knew what was lost. They reached out for each other in the dark.

Shadow

He reminded her of one of the vampires from *True Blood*, tall with high cheekbones and an intense stare. He overwhelmed the room. Something about the decisive way he moved around it too, getting things done. The rest home always smelled of antiseptic and death and the television was always on. His uniform fitted him a little too tightly, blue-collared shirt stretched over his torso and his trousers taut over his arse, which was a good arse, Anahera could tell. A large tā moko on his arm was nearing completion. It just needed a bit by the wrist, and it looked like it'd be a complete sleeve. If he remembered her, he wasn't letting on, though with masks on it was harder to recognise faces. 'There we go, Carol,' he said to her mum. 'Nice clean sheets, and you've got a visitor.'

'So where are you from?' Carol asked him.

Anahera put down her bag and looked around for a vase for the flowers she held in her other hand.

'Where did you go to school? Where do your parents live?'

'Hi Mum. Sorry I'm late.' She couldn't seem to harden herself, despite everything she now knew about dementia. She took a sandwich out of her bag, straightened up, and smiled. 'I just need to eat something.' And curl up in a corner to die. Plenty of time for that later, though.

Her mother lifted her face in Anahera's direction.

'You sound tired, love.' Her mother's hands were bruised again. She bruised so easily. 'Doesn't she?'

'I am a bit tired. Hi there,' she said.

'Hi.' He handed her a jar. 'Will this do the trick?'

She nodded. 'I brought you some daphne from the garden at work, Mum.'

'I could smell it coming up the hall,' Carol said. 'Lovely.' Her mum lost her sight three years ago, and perhaps because it happened gradually, took it in her stride. The onset of dementia two years ago is the reason she came here.

'You don't remember me, do you?' Anahera said, arranging the daphne in the jar. 'We know each other, don't we? From Eastern?' The poor bloke, it was a barrage of questions. She'd always asked a lot of questions – even as a kid. Carol used to invite a kid over to play in the morning, then arrange another one for the afternoon. Na would interview them in the tree house while her mum did the jobs.

He looked a bit embarrassed. He had recognised her. 'I wasn't sure. Anahera, isn't it?'

'It is, yeah. But everyone calls me Na. And you're—?'

'Shaun.'

'That's it, of course. I didn't think they'd be employing anyone new, given what's happening.'

'I'm a social worker. They've brought me in to support clients during the transition.'

'I hate every one of you cunts in here,' Carol said.

Na stayed quiet, but Shaun laughed loudly. Then Na laughed too, and it made her mother smile. Na couldn't bring herself to tell her mother she would have to move again. There was no point, not yet. Na's mum had no short-term memory and had made friends in the rest home, after a challenging move. They'd spent a lot of time looking for a suitable place and now had to find somewhere else, at short notice, in the middle of a pandemic.

They'd announced the closure via a pre-recorded webinar. On the screen behind Daryl, the manager, was a carefully arranged vista: a healthy fern, daylight through a partially open window. The walls of the real office were yellowed with age, something Na noticed each time she went in there to discuss her mother's care. Every few months since Carol moved here, the Board announced that they were working on getting a new building – then, there was no room in the budget. Despite the lovely backdrop, Daryl in his uniform black polo gave the impression of someone who would rather be anywhere than delivering this news that the home had to close. They'd been given six weeks.

Na said, 'You're getting out, Mum.'

'You are a great woman, a champion,' Carol said.

'Soon you'll be back in your big chair in my front room and we will be making marmalade, Mum.'

'Is it the season?' Carol gripped Na's hand tight.

'Yeah, I think so,' Na said, uncertainly.

'That is just what I want.'

Na parked in the driveway and left the engine going, reluctant to leave the warmth of the car. It was the 1.00 p.m. announcement and she waited to hear what was happening with the Levels. If they went up too much, she wouldn't be allowed to visit her mum. Today, like most days, there were a dozen more cases. The council phoned earlier to say her mum was entitled to carer support, but as there weren't any carers available, she wouldn't be getting any. It was the sort of autumn day that was already winter. She could see Jon through the window, at his workplace in front of the computer. She closed the car door hard, not a slam exactly but firmly enough that he'd hear it, which he did. He looked up; he was on a work zoom. Jon was a life coach. The pandemic had been good for the life-coaching trade – Na wasn't the only person who was lost this year – and he got to work from home.

Shadow was going mental at the door with the energy of an unwalked dog. Na went into the bathroom and washed her hands.

'The human mind is very simple,' Jon was saying. She'd heard this more than once.

When she came out, he was finished the call. She put her bag down on the floor by his chair and stood behind it. The shape of his back was beautiful. She touched his neck. The night her girlfriend introduced them, Jon told her how he'd been a sunglasses model for Kirks before he became a life coach. It had surprised Na that they got along. She'd just finished her final med school exams and had apologised for hardly keeping her eyes open.

'Did you hear the update?' She rifled through a pile of unopened bills.

He nodded. 'My noho marae will go ahead, then.'

'I'd like some fresh air. Shall we take Shadow for a walk before dinner? He looks like he could do with one,' she said pointedly. Hearing the word, Shadow thumped his tail. He was a large mongrel who Na inherited when her father died in Auckland Hospital three months ago. It wasn't written down anywhere, but her brother said he'd die too if he had to take Shadow. It was her brother who was paying for the rest home for their mum, so it felt like the least she could do. She and her brother weren't always on the best of terms She wondered if he paid for the home so he wouldn't feel guilty about living so far away.

'Can we eat first?' He clutched his stomach. 'I'm starving.'

She untucked herself and started to unbutton her uniform.

'Actually, babe, do you mind if I don't come for a walk?' he said. 'I'll make a start on dinner. But, also, can you deal with the dog hair on the bed? It's next level.'

'He might cry less if you took him out during the day, Jon. I didn't even stop for lunch today.'

'Okay, okay, relax, I'll do it,' he said.

She had started taking Shadow to bed with her – with them. If they left him outside, he would cry. Jon relented to him sleeping on the floor beside the bed, but Shadow just waited till Jon was asleep then jumped up. In the morning the duvet cover was always covered in dog hair and Na would promise to change it, but then would forget.

'Nothing to stop you changing it, you know,' she said.

Whenever he did any housework, he made a thing of it. When they met two years ago, he didn't care at all. He was low maintenance, which Na liked. His laugh was loud and sudden, and he was always cheerful. He was always bringing her things, a piece of polished glass or a stone the exact colour of her eyes.

'I just said I'd do it, babe. You really need to pace yourself,' he said, though it wasn't clear how she should do that. 'It's crazy to skip lunch.'

She thought about the work roster and how many hours she'd done that week. How it was an antisocial roster, how that didn't matter anymore now that the world was ending. Everyone was being more careful than usual, she had nowhere she needed to be, except now, here with Shadow. Everyone felt the loss, but it was worse for Shadow. She understood death more than most people, but since her father's death last month there seemed to be a question mark over everything. Normally, getting a dog pre-empted a baby. Na remembered how casual she was in the beginning.

'There's no rush. Once we have a kid, that'll be it.'

Whatever it was. The casualness had been replaced by three failed rounds of IVF, then a decision to give her body a break. And a five-month separation, after which they'd both admitted they missed each other. Living alone was surprisingly satisfying – if she tidied up the flat and then went out, it was still tidy when she got back. But she'd be forty-two next year – the cut off age for funded treatment. No doubt it was a mistake – she was too late, had waited too long. The baby wasn't coming.

Their flat was small but Shadow was big. Jon loved her but hadn't signed up for this. Maybe she was doing that thing people did when people died or left, of needing to change things up, make it different. The main consequence of having Shadow was that it made Na think about her father all the time. Shadow couldn't be left alone. She patted him, felt his ribs through his fur. How could it have happened so fast? Out of all the things that might have happened, why did life throw *this* at her?

The operation, to fix a complication from earlier bowel cancer surgery, was a success, but her father's recovery quickly became messy. Each day seemed to bring a new problem, and with community numbers of coronavirus infections rising, there was nothing to do but wait. They wouldn't let him drink, either. Her dad got better, then worse. Their phone calls, possible only with a nurse's help, were brief and often muddled.

One morning, Na woke to find a voice message from the hospital. He'd gone. All those years without him, then she'd lost him again. It didn't seem fair. She'd visited every so often over the years, but she hated being around him when he was drunk. Then a year ago, he'd decided to try and stop drinking.

He admitted himself to a Salvation Army rehab programme. They became friends.

The truth was she wanted to establish the sort of intimacy with Shadow that he'd had with her dad. Her dad took such good care of him, it was the least she could do.

'Just get to know each other,' she'd repeated. Jon had agreed to keep Shadow company during the day while she was at work. Shadow would curl up under Jon's desk.

'I'm not sure you should be sleeping with a hundred people,' she said. 'With Covid.' She removed the pillowcases. She didn't remember them being that filthy.

'Not *with*,' he laughed. 'If they're letting you into the rest home . . .'

'You could get a motel.' She was like the voice of Covid-19.

'Look, if you're really worried, I won't go.' He was really trying with te reo, he deserved credit for trying. She wished he'd just focus on everything else he was good at and quit humiliating her.

'Listen, by the time you come back, I'll . . .'

'You'll what? Have left your job? Have re-homed Shadow?'

Na wrapped her arms around Shadow. *Have put all your shit in boxes on the driveway* she didn't say. She knew what he wanted her to say. But she knew how attached Shadow was to her dad, and she was the next best thing.

'Listen, I found this.' He read off his screen. 'It is possible that the high prevalence of separation distress and other anxieties in the mixed-breed dogs is caused by a poor early-life environment and adverse experiences in life, as many mixed breed dogs in our data are likely rescues.'

They couldn't even give her dad a proper funeral. Her brother got angry, but Na was secretly relieved, in no doubt it would have been left to her to organise. Her father's ashes were in a cardboard box, in a bag, on their bedroom floor. She wanted to tell Jon to buck his ideas up. It wasn't as though he was allergic, and she worried about Shadow out in the cold. Jon's parents were still together and the way they treated her made her suspicious. If they'd met her in another context, they wouldn't have given her the time of day. They weren't snobs exactly; she just wasn't part of their world. Last week his mother had said, 'I can't imagine what you're going through', – a sentence Na was hearing a lot, and one that she rejected. You could imagine it if you tried hard enough.

She dressed in leggings and a sports bra. She grabbed an old T-shirt of her dad's that was huge on her, that smelled less and less of him. At the back door, she pulled on boots and a jacket. She put Shadow on the lead, and they walked to the end of the street, and through a gate onto a field. Somehow, making her body pretend she was in a good place tricked her brain into going along with it. Two kilometres away, her mum would be having her dinner in the home.

She let Shadow off. He ran ahead, although she was walking quickly. They did the same loop before work every morning. In the strange, shut-down landscape of lockdown, the empty streets made it feel as if everyone else was in mourning as well. She'd started thinking of it as her grief walk. Sometimes she sat for a while on a fallen tree, her breath clouding the air while Shadow explored, waiting to hear his name. The first lockdown was fine. Having no kid meant there wasn't any big deal with her many lives layering on top of each other in a confined space. She only had two lives, three at the most. At work and home, and out here, walking. She and Jon did the usual things to stay sane when confronted with seemingly endless periods of time and no real social life: jigsaws, taking too long to cook dinner, rewatching *The Wire*. But then something started to creep in, and then her dad got ill. She and Jon found new ways to irritate each other. Her feet seemed heavier on the walk back.

Later, they lay in bed. Jon reached out and touched her hand. She moved closer to him, and Shadow jumped up, pushing his nose between their faces.

'Na,' he said, taking his hand away. She looked into Shadow's soft eyes that seemed to care about her and know what she was going through and seemed to tell her it'd be okay. She was still loved.

'I'll put him out.'

'I've been thinking about what my dad said at our engagement party,' she said, getting back into bed, facing him. 'About marriage being a pointless thing.' She could hear Shadow panting through the door. Her dad's speech sounded like it would be great, then it wasn't. He finished by saying that when he married, in 1973, he hoped his children would never feel they had to participate in something so pointless.

Jon stared at her intently. 'Babe, can we talk about something else?'

'Okay, sorry.' She'd replayed that moment over and over, in her mind at that moment when she had told her dad to go fuck himself. The week before he died, they'd argued via text, something about how she never visited him anymore. She was unfair to him, too.

Now she and Jon lay in bed not talking. After a while, she slipped her hand under the elastic of his boxer shorts. He moaned appreciatively. He kissed her, gently at first, then a bit roughly, and she couldn't help feeling like he was marking his territory. Shadow barked.

He stopped kissing her. 'There must be somebody else who could—' he said.

'Jon,' she said. 'There isn't.'

They kissed again and he barked and when they stopped, he stopped barking.

'Fuck's sake, Na.'

'Oh, I'm sorry your sex life is being impacted,' she said. 'What, you don't fancy a threesome?'

'He's still bloody doing it,' Jon said. 'And no, I don't, thank you.'

'Who's still doing what?'

'Your dad. He was always winding me up.'

'Oh, come on.' It was true, her dad enjoyed showing Jon up. Not always in a mean way, exactly, although it was obvious in the little things he said that he thought Na could do better.

'I need to get to sleep. I'm obviously not getting laid tonight.' Then he said, 'I need you to promise me something. Promise we won't talk about the dog anymore.'

'This isn't working,' she said.

'No shit. I'm glad you realise it.'

'I don't mean Shadow. It's just not there. You're not here.'

He made suggestions, listened, then argued his part tactfully – slipping into life coach mode. As he laid out plans, discussed new strategies, Na realised something fundamental had shifted in her over the last few months, unnoticed by those around her.

She pulled the sheet over her head and lay very still. Should they talk about her mother coming to live with them? How did she explain it? It was like she was unmoored. You can't hold onto me, she wanted to say. Then she got up and went into the kitchen. She ate a handful of almonds for no reason, then poured an orange juice. She stood in front of the fridge looking at the photo of her mother, held there by a magnet which said, *The trees that are slow to grow bear the most fruit*. Her father gave her that when she graduated medical school. In the photo her mother was young and smiling. She was wearing a white top and cuddling a real koala bear. Her mother loved animals. Her mother loved many things; or did, before she got dementia – cooking, Bob Marley, all children, flowers, marmalade. Their determination to do the right thing by their mum meant in fact that they did the worst possible thing, moving her away from the home she knew well to a new and unfamiliar environment, and now moving her again, in the space of just two years.

Had she ever been this tired before? Everyone said grief was exhausting, but no one talked about the dread that came with knowing how tired she'd be again tomorrow. When she slipped back into bed, she found Shadow hiding under the duvet.

'Is she looking too thin?' Carol said to Shaun. 'I suspect she's not eating properly.'

'Mum,' she said, embarrassed. 'I'm just going to have a word with the manager.'

The walls of the office appeared even yellower.

'Daryl,' she said, 'do you have a minute?'

'Sure thing,' Daryl said. He closed the folder he was looking at and gestured to a chair by the door.

'Well,' she said, 'and you know I hate to do this, but—' Here it comes. 'Mum's got bruises again.'

Daryl's smile was a thin line.

'I just wondered if you knew anything about them.'

'As you might have heard, Na, we're really struggling to cover the shifts at the moment, and – did you meet Shaun, our social worker?'

'I'm not having a go, Daryl. It's very possible she's banging into things. I'm only letting you know.'

He nodded. 'Okay.'

'How's it going with the Board?'

'I've been here too damn long for this kind of nonsense. They can't pull this shit,' he said. 'Six weeks' notice! It's people's lives we're talking about. What's it like at the hospital?'

'We could use some help there, too.'

A sympathetic look crossed his face. Then he was telling her about empty buildings near the old train station, a new home they were planning on setting up there. He was dreaming, surely.

'We're watching some blocks down there,' he said. That was what he'd been doing yesterday, scoping out a new potential development. After all these months of isolation, with everything closing down, the need for a different life hadn't gone away: it was the opposite, people were clinging on.

She headed towards her mum's room in the annex, the only room available when they'd come to look. It was out of the original building and down an L-shaped extension on the back. She passed a stressed looking cleaner pushing a cart full of cleaning supplies, then another staff member helping an elderly man into a chair.

Today, she'd brought some audio books from the library. Shaun had had more tā moko work done on his wrist since her last visit: an immaculate koru unfurling against his brown skin. Where she came from, everyone was pale.

'The strangest thing has happened,' Carol said. 'I can't remember how I got here.' She looked through Na when she talked. She was restless, less agreeable than twenty minutes ago.

'Sol and I drove you,' Na said. 'We brought you here.'

When her mum first started to lose it, Na had wondered how she would survive in this new dimension. But in a lot of ways, her mum coped better than she did.

Carol looked relieved. 'I knew you'd know the answer,' she said.

'Are you close to your family?' Na asked Shaun.

'My mum passed suddenly five years ago. A lot of my friends and family thought I'd go off the rails, go back to drinking.' He paused. 'I still sometimes expect a text from her with a joke or the lyrics from an Eighties song.'

'Because it's everywhere, in the papers, on TV, it's a constant . . .' Na swallowed hard.

She told Shaun about the last time she saw her dad. 'It was in Auckland, during the first lockdown. I drove up there then drove him in for the op, but you know, Covid protocols, no visitors allowed on the ward of course. They told me to phone when we arrived at the hospital, and someone would meet us. But my phone wouldn't work in the carpark. It was emergency calls only. So, I had to run up two floors of ramps, dodging traffic, until I got some reception and could make the call.'

She realised she hadn't talked about it in months.

'I wasn't allowed to be with him the day he died either, say goodbye.'

She wondered if he'd be a selfish lover. She wanted him to be selfish. She imagined bringing her free arm up and touching his face with her fingers. Removing his mask and drawing a track down his jawline.

'I haven't cried since he died,' Na said. 'You can't cry when no one can hug you. Too awkward. Oh, I watched a film a couple of nights ago and I cried. But that was because of the film. He would have liked it.' She wanted to be somewhere else with him, an empty room or the beach or anywhere but here. She imagined a version of him, and one of her, not here in this stuffy room with her mother. Walking along the beach, hand in hand, fucking in the staff toilets. Generally, she felt numb, but around Shaun she had these feelings that manifested in fantasising about having sex with him. They were cautious around each other, as though pain was contagious, as though keeping a distance would make the loss smaller. Yet it was the nearness of things, of Shadow, her mum, that was all that mattered. It was the littleness. The compassion was in a nod, a smile, gentle tokens.

'Some days I'm okay,' she said. 'Then other days I go into total meltdown. Sometimes it feels like you're living in an alternate reality to others.'

He nodded.

'Did you?' she asked. 'Go off the rails?'

'Actually, the opposite happened and I just said to myself, I'm going to go for this, I'm going to jump off and see what happens.' He smiled. 'That's when I started my degree.'

'I miss our conversations,' Carol said, and gave a funny sounding laugh. 'He always talked so much in the morning. I can't stand the silence.' Na's parents separated when Na was three. Then there was the weird thing where her mum changed, her face clouding over. She realised she was having trouble understanding.

Na thought about what Jon had said in bed last night about her dad still winding him up, how easy it was to let him think she was just preoccupied with work. And she was, a lot of the time. He understood that her work was vital, that any conversations with colleagues were necessary. Shaun wasn't exactly a colleague, but when it came to Carol's care, it was important to be on the same page.

'I don't understand at all what is going on here,' Carol said. Suddenly, none of it made sense. 'What's happening here? How did I get here? What's happening?' She buried her face in her hands. This was how it was, something happened, and all of a sudden someone had to care for her, just like an infant. And she yelled things, swore, and sometimes scratched.

'Na is here, Carol,' Shaun said.

'You're all liars. That isn't Anahera. You think I don't know who Anahera is? Well, I do and that isn't her.' She stared at Na.

Na felt the air around them shimmer, as though they'd entered a new dimension. The tears welled up. This person was a different version of her mother.

Carol had never not known her. Na was shocked, and could see Shaun noticing that.

'When there's not much to talk about, we talk about you,' he said, looking her in the eye.

On Shaun's recommendation, Na stopped at the vet shop, where she bought a pair of rubber gloves, and some hypoallergenic dog shampoo.

She got into bed with Shadow. She reached for her phone to see if Jon had texted, but there were no new notifications.

Red Flags

Sabine and Jane sat on a bench at university, drinking from their water bottles. Sabine could feel her body catching the sun. Summer had arrived late, and everyone was out on the lawn, playing frisbee and scrolling through their phones on the new grass.

Sabine lifted her hair up like a curtain for a few moments, then let it settle back around her shoulders. 'Maybe I'll get my hair cut.' She kept leaving her water in the sun, so that when she went to drink it, it was hot.

'Perfect, considering the card I pulled for you this morning.'

In their first year at Victoria, Sabine and Jane had been hostel roommates. They hadn't known each other before, although they had friends in common, and Jane had made herself at home in Sabine's life. They'd moved into a flat in Aro Valley together a semester ago. Jane said it was meant to be. Jane was always looking for proof from the universe that she was on the right path.

'For the last time, I don't believe in that stuff,' Sabine said.

Jane tipped back her head and laughed. 'Get it cut for tonight then.'

'Tonight? What's—'

'Can I borrow those earrings you're wearing tonight? Haven't you been listening? I've been talking about the party for like a week. You haven't met Tristan's friends yet. I think it might happen tonight. We might hook up.'

'I haven't met all the members of the National Party either, but I know I wouldn't hang out with any of them,' Sabine said. It didn't sound like a jealous answer, but it was.

There was no clear moment when Sabine decided it was too late and she fancied Tristan as well. She usually went for brown boys and never rugby players. But then Jane had said Tristan had said he thought Sabine was attractive and to bring her to the party. Or something. But whenever they'd talked to him after rugby, he'd only looked at Jane, there was no denying that. Sabine wasn't sure exactly what Tristan said because she wasn't there. Jane was there and said that he mentioned that. Sabine envied how Jane could be anything at any moment, and, most of all, that she was okay with that.

'The card of decisions, the possibility of paths diverging,' Jane smiled, shifting her weight on the bench. 'And it's a full moon. It's like there's this kinetic energy in the air but no one can explain it.'

They had slept at opposite ends of the hostel room, a set of gauzy curtains splitting the space down the middle. When you shared a room with someone, you knew a lot about them. You knew what classes they had, their favourite spot in the library, which boys they liked. Whenever Sabine closed her eyes, that information was right there: What class does she have today? Where is she? All along Sabine had the sense that something was different about the way men treated Jane. It was as though there was a quiet centre of gravity in her, around which guys – no, people – orbited. She could feel the energy in the room change.

Sabine shook her head. 'I thought we had a pact not to fuck any rugby players.'

'I never said that! I'm taking fate into my own hands. It's

like when I read for friends, it's like I'm shuffling fates. Do you have any of those free condoms left? I just don't want to wake up ten years from now thinking I wish I'd given that a go.'

'I'm going to have to start charging you soon,' Sabine said.

She hadn't exactly lied. Mostly she hadn't told Jane what had happened with her ex because she hadn't told anyone. She'd let her believe she'd had great sex with her high school boyfriend, when it was probably the reason they hadn't lasted very long. She hadn't liked the way he touched her, as if he owned her. He was her first. After they broke up, he assaulted another woman. The hard thing, as Sabine saw it, was that something bad had happened to that woman and now everyone knew. And now when people thought of her, Sabine knew, they didn't really think of her. They thought about him and the things that he did. Or that she was a liar or someone who put herself in bad situations. The people who thought these things also said them online. She sometimes wondered if she was responsible.

The house was at the end of a street in Newtown, a few blocks from the bus stop. They felt the music before they heard it. Sabine's feet already hurt.

'Don't leave me by myself,' Sabine started to say, but Jane was practically dancing them both towards the house.

'This is it.' Jane inhabited her body with such ease. The driveway was full of cars and some people had parked on the grass.

Sabine let Jane go in first. She hung back, would have waited outside except she'd feel more stupid doing that.

Jane held the door for her. 'Come on,' she said.

They didn't know anyone, and Sabine drank the vodka

partly to hide from this, partly to forget her body. One of the other girls came over and introduced herself: Aisha. There were streaks of pink in her blonde hair. Jane introduced herself and Sabine and chatted to Aisha. The plastic chair pinched ridges into Sabine's thighs. Something in Jane always made Sabine aware of her own life and how little she'd done. It was hard to shake off, to not compare. But this had faded by the time Tristan appeared and with a sudden surge of confidence Sabine joined Jane in welcoming him and his friends into the group, standing up and making room at the table, telling them to pull up some chairs. Everyone sat down except Sabine because there weren't enough chairs now. Nobody noticed, or if they did, they didn't let on, crowding in at the table. She might as well not be there. They seemed to fill the room.

'You came, nice one.' He was already drunk.

Sabine could smell aftershave. His cigarette made orange dots in the night. Everyone said their names – Shay, Anthony, Markus, Tristan. Tristan didn't understand where she said she was from. He bent forward at her with a frown and shouted 'Where?' when she said Taranaki, so at some point she said New Plymouth instead and Markus said, 'Oh, she means the Naki.' There were only four of them, including Tristan, but they made enough noise for more. They'd won the rugby and Tristan shouted the score, 18–15, and shouted again with laughter. He leaned on the table, his blond hair falling over his forehead. He drained his glass.

Tristan spoke to Jane and Jane laughed. 'Let's get you drunk,' he said.

Jane was already a bit pissed. There was a joke, but Sabine didn't hear it, only laughed when the others did. Jane always laughed in the right places. Sabine felt her face go red, even though she didn't know for sure what it meant. She took out her phone for something to do. Tristan put his arm around the back of Jane's chair and leaned back on his own. He had pale skin, freckles on his scalp.

'What are you studying?' he asked her.

'Theatre.'

'What, like acting?'

Sabine couldn't believe he'd asked that. She went looking for a chair but there wasn't one. They had taken a lot of the furniture out of the living room to make space for, what, a dancefloor? There were lots of people in the living room now, standing around. A handful of people vaped by the doorway. She didn't want to go back and have to stand, or worse, have someone suggest she sit in their lap. The room was too bright. She went upstairs. She was looking for distractions. When she got to the top of the stairs, a guy was standing with the bathroom door open, pissing into the toilet. He was wearing a white singlet. She'd seen him at the hostel. His name was Cy. The reason she remembered his name was because Jane had secretly organised a cake for her birthday last year and it was him who'd brought it into the dining room. He was the kitchen hand. Every year, a third-year student took the kitchen job and got free accommodation in return. He was shy, smiled a lot, didn't say much. Sabine knew his sister, an outgoing and gregarious first-year, seemingly her brother's total opposite. He washed his hands, then walked out onto the landing. Around his neck was a delicate gold chain with a cross.

'Oh, hey,' she said.

'I know you, don't I?' he said.

In the moment she had options, she could have gone back to the lounge, but it felt like giving in. She wanted to see if it was something or nothing.

'Yeah, I was in the hostel.'

He held up a bottle. 'Want some?'

She took the bottle and drank. It burnt as it went down and made her cough. She made herself drink more. What was it Jane had told her? The possibility of paths diverging. Jane had this stupid belief in fate. Last month, Jane had only realised what day it was after she'd gotten into a big fight with her mother. She had checked her journal and her calendar. She couldn't believe it. The full moon. What Sabine didn't say to Jane was that she sometimes longed for more options too, and yet, despite this, she was scared of what it might mean. He had nice eyes. She tried to work out how old he was.

'What's it like working at the hostel?' She just wanted to make this thing happen. He seemed like he wanted the same thing. There was something easy about him.

'It's just a job,' he said. 'Free rent.' They drank some more. 'What are you studying?'

'Is it okay if we kiss instead of talk?' she said. He nodded and she leaned in and kissed him on the mouth. They kissed for a few minutes. She pushed his mouth open with her tongue. He was a good kisser. 'There's a bedroom down the hall that I bet no one ever uses.'

He laughed, surprised. 'What?'

'I promise not to do anything that you don't want me to do,' she said. She would fuck him and if she hated it, she'd stop. She was in charge. 'My night isn't going anywhere. Let's go.' If it was bad, she could just avoid him.

His dick was already hard. They stood in the dark bedroom, kissing some more.

'You got a condom?'

They took off their clothes, fumbled with each other's bodies.

'What do you want?'

She told him what she liked and how she wanted it. The bed was unmade. Straddling him, she leaned down to kiss him while she fucked him in a steady rhythm. He moaned, gripped her hips, pulling her into him, then pushing away. It was like there were two of her, like her upper and lower body were separate or something.

Afterwards, he sat on the edge of the bed and pulled on his shirt. She wanted to remember the way he looked right then, with the scrape of his chin still on her skin and the feeling of something clicking into place. She leaned over and kissed his bottom lip, then the top.

'Fuck, sorry, I have to go,' he said. 'My parents are in town. Do you want to hook up later? There's something on at the club.'

Sabine couldn't see Jane, but she could hear her on the other side of the room, in a group of mostly guys. So many people populated Jane's life. Sabine wanted to go over to her, nudge her, tell her about Cy. The party was really getting started, there were people everywhere now.

'Are you an actress too?' Markus said from somewhere.

'No.' She didn't want to stay but something was preventing her from leaving.

'I can't figure you out, Naki Girl,' Markus said.

She heard Jane say, 'Where have you been, Been's?'

'Hey, come talk to me. Naki girl.' It was Markus again.

Sabine hated confrontation. Sometimes she lay in bed at night, going over her day, and all the things she should have said, but didn't. She pushed through the crowd of people around Jane. Jane was drinking vodka and something pink.

'What was all that about?' Jane said.

'Oh. Nothing.' Sabine couldn't be bothered getting into it.
'Didn't sound like nothing,' Jane said.

Jane was wrapped up in whatever was going on with
Sabine and Markus, none of which was that interesting. It
felt like she didn't care about Sabine's news.

'I bumped into someone I know,' Sabine said.

Sabine ran into Aisha and the other girls when she was thinking
of going home and they were loud and friendly and wanted
to know where she was from. When she said Taranaki, they
said cool, and Aisha was from here, but the rest were from
Auckland. They invited her for drinks. Sabine missed Jane,
then, but decided to stay for one. They sat on the balcony.
Everyone agreed she couldn't leave yet; the night was young.

It was later when Jane told Sabine she wasn't going home with
her. The party was almost over. Tristan had asked her to go
to another party with him. She was sitting on the arm of his
chair. Sabine could see the shift in her. Her movements were
slower, eyes rolling into focus. She slipped across onto his lap,
letting him kiss her. The kissing went on for a while. When
she pulled back, opened her eyes, he said something to her
that made her face go red.

'There's a party,' Jane said again. 'I'll see you at home.'

There was something different in Tristan's eyes when
he looked at Sabine. He swigged the last bit of the bottle.
Somehow in that moment, it was clear Sabine had never been
the girl he wanted. She was angry at Jane again, wanted to
tell Tristan she was the one he didn't know, wanted to know.
Markus was talking, but she couldn't hear the words. Tristan
squinted at her.

'Remind me again.'

'Sabine.'

'Oh, right.' Tristan sounded vague, as if trying to recall something he'd heard about her. 'You've changed your hair.'

'I got it cut.'

Jane stood up and wobbled off towards the bathroom. People saw but everyone was ignoring it because no one wanted to see that. Sabine went after her and held her hair while she threw up.

They went outside. Some of them talked quite loudly until they saw Sabine and Jane then their voices dropped. Nothing had really been said.

'You all right there, Janey?' Tristan said, grinning.

They weren't in a hurry, but it was as though they were waiting for something, an event. They were pleased with themselves. They spoke in pairs or as a whole and there was laughing. Then Markus and Anthony had an argument about something someone had said. Jane was sitting on the footpath now, head in her hands. Shay went inside and came back with four beers and handed them out.

'You can't stay there,' Sabine said, sitting down beside her. She should make her come with her. Of course she should. Shay rolled a cigarette and Tristan vaped, making big clouds in the air.

'It's all right,' Tristan said. 'We'll look after her.'

Sabine looked at him. It was like there was no way Jane was going home with her. Nothing to worry about. Tristan wanted everything to be clear, no misunderstanding. There couldn't be. Things had reached their natural conclusion; Jane was going with them. She wondered what he wanted, whether he wanted her to stop whatever was going to happen. She watched them drinking their cans, watching her. Shay ground his cigarette into the footpath. When Sabine stood up, she put her hands on the car to steady herself.

'She's wasted.'

'Such a judgy bitch,' Tristan said. But he'd begun to smile a little. His face was flushed. 'Are you just a bit jealous, Sabine?' They could say anything, and they would. Jane didn't know them at all, not really. 'Jealous bitch.' It would have made Sabine laugh, except that it was so shit. Someone laughed so hard they coughed and sounded as though they'd hurt themselves. There's nothing like that happening here. There's no problem.

'Your wife Janey doesn't want to go home with you. She wants to be told what to do. Do you wish we'd fuck you, Sabine?' That was Tristan. There were some people taking photos out on the balcony. Music was coming from Markus's phone. Every one of them had their tops off. Her eyes got that hot feeling.

'How do you know what she wants?' Sabine said.

'I don't think that's what he meant,' Shay said. 'That's not what he said.'

'Because she told me. Look, we're all friends here, aren't we?' Tristan said.

Jane leaned over and took the beer from Sabine's hand. 'You're drunk,' she said. 'Go home. You're so sweet to me, Beens.'

It was like they didn't believe her. They refused to see what she saw. They couldn't even see how they were playing out a story right there: Jane on the footpath, Sabine watching them, the music, the other guys, car lights shining at the house. They'd made their point: nothing here but us. Still, when she told them Jane was too drunk to go, it was like they thought she was having a joke at their expense.

'I'll come with you.' Jane said no, she was fine, and she was going, and Sabine wasn't. It seemed an answer good enough, although Sabine knew, somehow, that it wasn't.

And this would be a story to tell in the morning, sitting under Sabine's duvet in their room, looking out the window and saying it was a good party, but you nearly didn't make it home. Or Monday on campus, sitting in the noisy hub with coffee, telling the story of how Jane had almost swum out too far. How Sabine had to pick her up off the footpath. It was a close one, she'd tell the others. She didn't want to come home with me. Better be more careful next time, someone would probably say, just as well Sabine was there to look out for you, and Jane might laugh and say, well, I know that now. And everyone would go quiet for a moment, thinking about it.

Except Sabine was pretty sure the conversation with Jane didn't happen, that she hadn't looked out for her. She remembered the cold concrete of the footpath against the backs of her legs. The look on Tristan's face, his laughter. The vodka spilling down Jane's chin. Jane, if she noticed at all, didn't care. Music, and voices colliding in the cold night air. There wasn't any use trying once it had gone that way. As Tristan jumped in the back seat with Jane, he told Sabine to text her later and pick her up and something else and, weeks later, Sabine had wondered how Jane might feel about being in a car, an enclosed space, with guys she didn't really know. There were four in the back, including Jane. You knew and didn't know. Sometimes her whole life felt like that. As if it was a way of coping. The headlights from the road had passed over Sabine's face as they drove Jane away from her and disappeared.

Still no Jane when she woke up at 5.30 a.m. Vomiting into the toilet, she thought – I left Jane. In the bathroom, while she brushed her teeth, she thought about all the previous times they'd gone out together, and about last night. How

Jane had looked, face flushed, as she turned to Sabine and said go home.

Sabine rolled over in bed and held her phone inches from her face. She scrolled on, through a few photos of the party and someone's Oriental Bay sunset, before seeing it at the top of the screen: a new video from Tristan, posted only a couple of hours ago. She pressed play.

She watched the six-second video three more times to confirm it was Jane. Jane's face wasn't visible. Sabine sat on the edge of the bed, looking at her phone. She called Jane and it went to voicemail. She needed to come home. Sabine tried to tell her, and she didn't listen. All the things she'd thought could happen had happened. She was that person that left her friend in a bad situation. This was going to be very bad.

Jane got back at 6.30 a.m. She looked the same, which shouldn't have been surprising. Except her hair was loose and it was strange to see it like that as she always wore it tied up. She said she'd taken an Uber, that Tristan paid for it. It was hard to tell whether it was blood or red wine on her top at first. What Sabine thought about mostly, while Jane was making the coffee, was whether she should tell her about the video. Jane interrupted her thoughts frequently, trying to get her to talk about Cy or the club or anything else. She was waving her hands around like she often did when she was angry even though she didn't sound angry. From the video, it seemed clear that she was out of it and hadn't noticed that she was being recorded. Sabine had watched it enough times to be sure of that. But it wasn't clear if Jane knew. And whether Sabine should tell her. Jane talking gave her an excuse not to talk. The headache had now settled at her temples, pressing at the back of her skull, around her neck.

'Do you need some painkillers?' Jane asked, seeing her face. 'What time did you leave the party?'

Sabine shrugged but her eyes were flicking around. 'Don't know,' she said. 'You remember much?'

Jane shook her head. 'Not really.'

When Jane offered Sabine a cup, she realized she'd been holding her breath and exhaled slowly, afraid Jane would notice. She shook her head. 'I've already taken some painkillers, thanks.'

Jane nodded.

Sabine met her eyes and wondered again if she remembered anything. She could put off dealing with it until she had to. 'I just feel really sick. I'm going to lie down for a bit,' Sabine said.

She put her hand on Jane's shoulder as she walked past her. She didn't look at Jane when she spoke, but it was like the words passed completely over her anyway. But then Jane reached for her hand. Sabine hadn't prepared what to say. She could say the truth about the video, but that could mean making things worse. Jane's life had blown up, and she didn't know it yet.

'I tried to get you to come with me,' Jane said. She looked at Sabine, like she was looking for some recollection. 'It was a crazy night. We went to another party.'

'What are they doing?' As if Sabine should know. Sabine didn't know how to answer. 'But what are they doing?' Jane asked this question over and over after she watched the video. It was like everything hinged on what Sabine said. Sabine considered her answer. How did she explain it? She had to say something. They watched the video, then Jane turned and looked at Sabine. 'That isn't me.' Jane would have stayed with her, Sabine thought later. She wouldn't have left her. And she realised that this feeling of guilt was familiar, and she thought she might be sick.

'I tried to make you come home with me.' If she'd come home, they wouldn't be here now. Sabine thought about being asleep in bed that morning, and now – they were here.

'That isn't me,' Jane said. It was the second time she'd said it. It didn't make it any better, nothing was going to make this better. Sabine wondered whether anyone would forgive her for this, whether they would understand. She doubted it. But doubt no longer seemed like a good enough reason for not doing something. There were plenty of red flags that night. Some were small, subtle things that didn't seem right, other things less subtle. Sabine had brushed them aside.

Jane looked around the room, as though searching for something left undone. 'Please,' she said. 'Let's talk about something else.' It was hard to hear the truth.

'Your head is bleeding.' The blood was matted in Jane's hair. The situation was all frozen in Sabine's mind now, like they were all still standing on the footpath outside the party, and Tristan saying *We're all friends here aren't we.*

Jane's head was bleeding and she remembered banging it on a coffee table. There were things she remembered and things that weren't the same. It was a room, with two sofas and a big television. A coffee table with a few mugs on it and a magazine. The room didn't have windows, maybe a basement room. This morning, Tristan and Markus were sitting on another sofa. Tristan helped her find her phone. Talking about it with Sabine made it more certain. She told Sabine what little she could remember: about the grass and sticks under her feet, being made to drink some water.

'Listen. Can we just go to After Hours?' because by then, Sabine had noticed the blood.

'Things that get deleted don't count,' Jane said, and then, because Sabine was giving her that stare, 'I mean things that mightn't even have happened don't count.'

The trip to After Hours was short but took ages. Sabine's head was clearing a bit. There were some questions the nurse kept coming back to. How much alcohol had Jane had? How much alcohol had Sabine had? Try to be clear, he said. And Sabine could see Jane was trying. But when Sabine talked, it was somehow not what she'd intended. Not once, Sabine realised, had she thought of Cy. They had hit it off pretty well. But she kept wishing things were different, wishing they weren't here now. And hooking up with Cy felt like part of that.

'I think we should go to the police,' Sabine said. They stood outside After Hours. The nurse had put some glue on Jane's head. She was lucky not to need stitches.

'How long were you upstairs with Cy for?' Jane said. She was smiling.

'I don't know exactly, maybe thirty minutes.'

'And what was I doing when you came down?'

'Everyone seemed quite drunk then. Markus was a bit of a dick. The guys were talking about leaving.'

'I don't remember.' Jane wrapped her jacket tightly around herself. She wasn't smiling now. 'I don't buy it.'

'You were drinking vodka and grapefruit, I think. I was on the balcony with Aisha and those girls – it gets a bit vague after that.'

'I sat on the footpath; it was cold. I tried to get you to come with me.'

It hadn't started that way, although there were signs. Were there signs? Sabine asked herself. 'Jane, we should go to the police about the video. That's fucked.'

'I need to lie down. I just want to sleep. There's no video, Beens,' Jane said. 'And I can't remember what I don't remember.' She could do what she wanted, she would consider her options.

The people at the station told Sabine they really needed Jane to make a statement. That night Jane went home to her parents' house.

Today was sunny. Sabine changed into a pair of loose fit jeans and a hoodie and set off for the library. She needed to find a new flat because the landlord had put rent up again. She had long since changed her route into town – instead of taking the narrow path through the trees, she took the main route. The inner Wellington streets that had seemed cute before didn't now, and even Cuba Street had lost its charm. Everywhere reminded her of Courtenay Place. It wasn't for her. No more getting pissed and walking home. It was all because of Jane. She tried to put herself in Jane's shoes. Jane's name was spoken on campus for a few weeks, then repeated. A lot of people saw the video. Jane's name trended on Twitter and Sabine's phone vibrated with phone calls and emails and text messages. Then people moved on. Tristan and Markus and the others hadn't meant anything, not really. A car tooted as it drove past. She didn't recognise the driver. The weekends kind of sucked without Jane. She told herself all the time she should have helped her.

At the library, Sabine sat at a table by a big window. She looked online for a flat then wrote another email to Jane that she wouldn't send. *You didn't do anything wrong,* she began, then deleted it. She read the earlier drafts at night on her phone when she couldn't sleep.

Someone had left the paper on the table, and she was

halfway through the magazine section, when she felt a tap on her shoulder.

'Mind if I join you?' It was Aisha.

'Sure.' Sabine didn't want to chat, but she smiled at Aisha anyway.

'Hey,' she said. 'Wow, that was bad at that party, eh? How's Jane doing?'

She couldn't pretend that things were normal. Sabine said, 'She left,' then added, 'I wouldn't really know.' Seeing Aisha brought the whole thing back. Sabine started to lose it a bit.

'Those guys,' Aisha said. 'Have you talked to her?'

Sabine thought of the way she talked to Jane before she left and rubbed her face. 'She doesn't reply,' she said. 'I can't stop thinking that if she was my best friend, you know, I'd have tried harder that night – to get her to come home with me.' She breathed in, she was talking too fast.

Aisha took a packet of tissues out of her bag and handed them to Sabine.

'But she wasn't. So, I let her do what she wanted to do.'

She tried to write an application for a flat. There was a 1.00 p.m. viewing on Aro Street. She'd go to that. A man stopped by where she was sitting to ask her for directions to the art gallery, touching the table she sat at. She wanted to stab his hand with her pen. She couldn't tell Jane about these things. She made herself go to the park. It took more energy than was justifiable. Just to look at some trees. It was one of those Wellington days where a grey sky brightens any colour and someone had found a child's pink sunhat and put it on top of a post. Sabine pulled her hood forward over her face.

Sweet on the Comedown

It was dark when the alarm went off. Pania could see the glow of Viv's cigarette out the window. Her back ached and she needed a piss. Viv never smoked unless she was having a drink, but she'd been drinking more than usual. They'd driven for four hours last night, across the flat land of the Desert Road until darkness reached around the bends in the road and they lost sight of the mountains in the distance, and they couldn't tell south from north anymore. A woman with a torch who introduced herself as Helena, the head gardener, had met them at the gate and taken them down to the free accommodation.

In the bathroom, Pania dressed in the clothes she had taken off the night before. It was a few minutes before 6.00 a.m. Morning didn't suit them, but they needed this job. They needed money and a routine was going to help them. Now that they were here, she wanted to get to work as soon as possible. The sooner they started the sooner they could leave.

Viv waited outside, where there were more buildings, identical A-frames in an inward-facing circle. Her hair was tied up in a messy bun, eyes expressionless. How had the others wound up here? Were they running away too? Pania wondered. She felt as if her Wellington life didn't exist. Viv had cried when Pania told her and cried harder when Pania said sorry for not being better and Viv had looked at her with eyes that had a haunting all of their own.

The special effects party had been on the Saturday of the long weekend. Viv had a urinary tract infection and Pania offered to sell her ticket. She went around to get it on Friday after work, but Viv was off at the chemist. While she waited for Pania to get back, Brett asked her if she wanted to make some extra cash. It sounded easy enough and Pania was so broke, she just ended up saying yes. Brett would throw in two free pills as well.

The pills were strong. Pania shifted most of the first bag by about 10.00 p.m. and could see the change in people. She must have taken her pill around midnight.

She found the woman when she went outside for some air. Something glittery stuck out. Pania knelt to pick it up and it was a boot. Then a leg. The woman was wedged down between a staff trailer and an inflatable castle, almost out of sight. Her dress had ridden up and there was a hole in her tights. Pania couldn't see her face because her hair was covering it and she was jammed hard up against the trailer.

She went to find Brett. He was standing at the front watching the kapa haka, all teeth and smiling. He'd had his torso painted to look like a leopard. He came to look, and they talked about what to do. Pania wanted to call an ambulance, but Brett said she was overreacting.

'We're high,' he said, 'it's late, she's not going anywhere.' They put a tarpaulin over the girl and left her where she was. But Pania stopped before they reached the gates.

'We need to get some help. We can't just leave her like that.' She tried to tell him. It wasn't right. They were high and scared, but it wasn't right. She started walking back.

Brett had grabbed her shoulders roughly, turning her back towards the entrance. 'Don't make a scene, sweetheart. That's not so hard, is it? Just go home, Pania.'

Pania was waiting in Miramar for the night bus when she heard sirens.

'What were you thinking?' Viv asked her and Pania found she couldn't say, except that she got scared and it was a terrible lack of judgement. Pania wasn't sure Viv would speak to her again, but when she woke the next morning Viv had found the job online and packed a suitcase and a couple of bags. She didn't even bother to lock the front door of the flat. Brett had already disappeared.

They crossed the grounds of the estate, wearing their boots and carrying their work shoes, black flats purchased in a clearance sale in Ōtaki on the way here. The ad said they needed regulation shoes. The building they approached was three stories tall and made of stucco painted blue, brick red and cream. It looked like an iced cake. There was nobody else around. Smoke rose from two chimneys on the shingled roof. They changed their footwear outside the side door, leaving their boots underneath a bush.

The dining room was like a ballroom and brightly lit. The light was coming from a huge crystal chandelier hanging in its zigzag frame, and smaller ones surrounding it. The room was crowded with tables, all laid with white linen cloths and set silver. French doors opened out onto a terrace with tables and chairs. Pania and Viv paused inside the doorway, taking in the room's size and brightness.

Before they could do anything, one of the doors on the far wall swung outwards into the room, revealing the woman from last night, Helena, wearing a Swanndri over her uniform. She made no noise as she crossed the room towards them, back and forth between the many tables, no path being clear amongst them. She took them down a hallway and showed them into a small room, with a table at one end and two armchairs. Two more women sat at the table, having cereal.

'Just coffee please,' Pania said and saw glances. One of the women pointed to a silver urn at the end of the table. Pania poured two cups of coffee and passed one to Viv. She took one armchair and Viv sat in the other. As Pania sat down she caught her reflection in a mirror above the fireplace. There were bags under her eyes.

One of the women spoke.

'Guessing you're the newbies. I'm Anna and this is Kara.' They were both much younger than Pania and Viv, with pale skin and extremely blonde hair.

'We're locals. We work here every summer,' Kara said. 'Just over the university break and help out the Vandenbergs during the silly season.'

The Vandenbergs were the owners of the estate and were siblings. Kara pointed to a large, framed portrait of them at one end of the room, too big for the space.

'The whole family are away in Europe at the moment,' she said. Tobias Vandenberg was tall with blond hair. Katrin looked stronger than her little brother, with her short crop and heavy features.

Pania stared at the painting.

'Are you staying in the A-frames too?' Viv said.

Kara shook her head. 'We don't stay onsite. Our families have had farms in the area for generations.'

'Which one's Viv and which one's Pania? Are you Pania?' Anna spoke to Viv, pronouncing Pania's name like 'pain'.

'It's Pania,' Pania said. She drew out her name. 'Pa-ni-a.'

Anna wrote their names on white card.

'It can be hard to tell everyone apart,' Kara said. 'Never

mind remembering names.' Kara's skin had the waxy appearance of an old doll.

'You're not from around here, are you?' asked Anna, passing them the name badges. She spoke like someone twice her age.

Pania was about to say no when she remembered she'd been born near here.

Viv tapped her phone. 'No reception.'

'No internet,' said Kara.

'It's not like it used to be here,' said Anna.

'Since the freak siblings came?' Pania said, half joking and Anna looked at her like this was a thing you couldn't mention.

Viv's eyes filled up. 'How will my boyfriend get in touch with me?'

Pania put her arm around Viv but felt relieved. Brett's texts always came in a rush. In the space of ten minutes, he could send nearly thirty, and Viv always panicked, trying to reply to them. This always happened when she went anywhere without him. He'd want to know where she was, who she was with, when she'd be back. This was one place he couldn't follow her, the one time he had no say on what she wore, how she did her hair, what she said. But Pania knew it wouldn't be that simple, not for Viv.

Kara shook her head. 'It's for our own good. We're protected now, from that uncle we hate, that friend we thought was okay, and that toxic chat group.'

Before Pania or Kara could speak, a buzzer sounded. The others stood up.

'Shift's started,' said Anna.

The guest rooms were huge and luxurious, the most expensive of them facing the mountain. Anna got them some colonial style uniforms out of a storeroom and they put them on. It was strange to be wearing new shoes and scratchy clothes and it was as though they moved differently. They spent ages looking at themselves in the mirror.

For a week or so, they got to know the routine. The cleaning was dull and repetitive. Cleaning all morning, then lunch. Lunch was always meat stew that Viv and Pania couldn't eat. At work, everything smelled and tasted of meat, even the salad. Pania and Viv had never been thin, but they were losing weight now. Every day after lunch they made afternoon tea for the guests who arrived on a bus – cucumber sandwiches and scones with jam and cream, and huge silver urns of tea. When nobody was looking, they would go into the walk-in chiller and stuff their faces with scones and sandwiches. Fresh bread arrived daily on a truck. The owners went hunting and came back with wild boar and quail and deer. Sometimes, all the cupboards in the kitchen were open and Pania and Viv stole rolled oats and jelly crystals, anything sugary or filling.

The other women were different from Kara and Anna. They shared whatever food they had with Pania and Viv and they worked outside, landscaping the vast gardens. They'd been jammed together in the circle and Pania couldn't work out the connection between them all, other than feeling that the parts were inseparable, inside her.

Helena next door, with the photos of her teenage daughters lining the windowsills. Her boredom as a housewife had led to bidding on the market and losing everything. She checked her phone constantly, even though there wasn't any reception.

Rae used to be in politics, the others said. She'd had a salary and houses in Auckland and Wellington. It wasn't easy to imagine her striding the corridors of the Beehive, talking at press conferences. She showed Pania photos of herself wearing designer suits.

Then there was Simone, a lawyer. 'What part of the country are you from? And through what misfortune did you end up in this shithole? It would be easy to feel sorry for Helena. But what would be the use in that?'

The A-frame women all talked about the Vandenbergs unkindly and often. Pania wondered if it was so they didn't have to talk about themselves. At first, they wouldn't give anything up. There were the stories they told about the owners and the job, then there were things they were not telling. Pania knew this because of Viv, things she wouldn't say, even to Pania. They might take months to come out, even years.

The nights before their day off Pania and Viv stayed up till dawn.

'Where shall we go when this is over?' said Pania.

'Somewhere warm, up north.' Viv grew up further north. She liked to show off, telling people she didn't have shoes till she was ten. 'Maybe even overseas.'

Pania knew in Viv's mind Brett was with them, sharing a bed with them, legs entwined. Viv would forgive everything because he was there. He had been in and out of Viv's life for almost as long as Pania could remember – since high school, when he rode a motorbike and had those stupid white boy dreadlocks. Whenever he got tired of sneaking around, he came back to Viv, but she always disappointed him with her wanting. Viv was better without Brett.

Food was a problem. Sometimes Pania would see Viv gazing at the venison stew or the sausage rolls. They ate a lot of oats and sugar. Occasionally, there was a block of tofu. They smuggled food back to the A-frame whenever they could. They grew muscles in their skinny arms.

There was no internet, but there was a river along whose banks Pania and Viv found fallen trees, smooth stones, the bleached bones of rabbits or deer. They felt rich here somehow; they had all that land to play on, they had the A-frame – its dark room, its fireplace, its fading wallpaper, and floorboards fastened with nails. Viv no longer talked about going home, seeming less disturbed and more in control. Their days were a rhythm of cleaning, waitressing, sleep, stealing food and saving money. It was easy for them to imagine that their new life was here. Viv started wearing makeup again. Their hair grew long, and Helena cut it in the staff kitchen, the offcuts of Pania's black hair falling on top of Viv's brown.

Kara clutched her blonde ponytail and stroked it.

'You're not having this, it's mine.' Anna repeated her words. Pania shrugged.

Sometimes guests left things behind: underwear, half a bottle of wine, a silk scarf. They sifted through the lost property box. Nobody ever seemed to come back to claim items, so they started taking what they found in the rooms.

'There's a party,' Rae said. 'Come if you want.'

The other women had made a place on the flat ground up from the river, amongst some big rātā trees. There was a fire pit dug into the ground, and further up the bank, the dirt had been carved out to make a long bench. It looked well established, like they'd been coming here for years. They sat on the bench drinking from cans or stood by the fire talking. Every now and then someone would throw a bit of wood on the fire. Everyone was in jumpers and scarves, fingerless gloves. Often, they would use a word Pania didn't know and she wondered if they liked that she and Viv didn't understand. The more they listened, Pania knew the language was inside her, waiting to be ignited.

'I reckon it could all be a big hoax,' Helena said in her singsong voice. 'Making us think we chose to come here, that we get a clean slate if we toe the line. What's the bet I'll be here this time next year. This is where they keep all the frauds and con artists. Just you wait and see. I'll be here next Christmas.'

Next Christmas. That's ages away, Pania thought. She looked at the fire. She must be joking. Even if it were possible, Pania couldn't keep this up that long. As soon as they'd earned enough money they could bail, couldn't they? Viv was already in a better mental state.

Simone had had an argument with one of her clients whose housing development project had been opposed by iwi. They wanted their land back and Simone wanted them to get it back. She'd sat on a rock on the road, refusing to move. The client had sued Simone for a conflict of interest.

'If I'd known what I was letting myself in for I'd never have come out here,' Rae said. She seemed to be talking more to herself than to Pania. 'I'd have stayed in the city. Why did you come here, anyway?'

Pania opened her mouth to reply but Rae wasn't finished. 'It's not like most of us haven't done worse.' Pania looked past her and down to the river rushing past. She wanted to say it out loud to someone other than Viv. She was beginning to wonder if everything in her life was now being funnelled through what happened at the party. She was plagued with regret about leaving that woman, angry at herself for having the chance to have made the right decision but making the wrong one.

'I don't think about helping people understand,' said Rae. 'Sometimes folks get it. Sometimes they don't. That can't be my concern. I'd drive myself in circles. I can't and won't do that. Because I have somewhere to go – and circles won't get me there.'

Her words slurred a bit as she talked. Pania had asked why she left parliament.

'Basically, I lied, then told the truth about the lie.'

Pania could feel Viv's arm against hers. That didn't seem like much. The thing about men like Brett was they never told the truth. He was always telling Viv it wasn't healthy to be so emotional. There were a lot of murmured conversations and texts not meant for her.

'I mean the government made it into a fucking public scandal!' said Helena. 'Hardly as though Rae's the first person not to get their young life right.'

'Now I'm paying the price,' Rae laughed. 'Once the blood was in the water, the sharks – they came for me.'

'He went on the radio with his rose-tinted glasses. Rumbling tummies getting louder by the day and he said he couldn't back up the research. Poured the money into the casino. It wouldn't have mattered what you said, you were done. What you did isn't as bad as what he did, but he's still the fucking Deputy Prime Minister,' said Simone. 'And so this is the only place that'll employ us – no references, no CVs. No questions asked.'

'It's about what you're trying to hide. Do you understand?' Rae said. 'That's the reason you're here, the reason we're all here.'

Pania felt the tears gather at the back of her throat. She looked at Viv.

Rae said, 'You thought you chose to come here, eh? Yeah, we all did. We all answered that fucking ad. But I should tell you that the further into things I've gone, the more I've found myself forming opinions.'

'It's okay,' said Helena, before Pania could tell them what she'd done. That she and Brett had left a woman to die. That she'd left her there and gone home. 'It's possible to make yourself new.'

After a few more cans, everyone talked freely. They showed her photographs on their phones, of the men involved in each scandal, the dirty politicians, Helena's ex, Simone's client. They zoomed in on their faces and throats and belt buckles. Pania never would have imagined that all the other women were here for the exact same reason. They'd all done things.

'I'll tell you everything,' Pania said as they gathered around, Simone, Rae and Helena all leaning forward.

'It would kill me if anything happened to Brett,' Viv said. 'I've always said I would put my hand in the fire for him.'

Hand in the fire. Kill me. Pania looked at the other women, waiting to catch a slight curve of a smile on someone's face, a hint that this was all happening in her imagination. But no, they were still looking at her, to her.

'Tell them, Viv. Tell them about the woman at the party.'

'People are never surprised when men like him go missing,' Rae said.

'We've all made poor judgements before. It's like if you've been here long enough, you kind of see and then you step too far like that and you go, "shit",' said Helena.

'I'm not the same as you,' Viv said.

Rae tipped her head on one side.

It hadn't occurred to Pania that while she was figuring all this out, Viv might have reached her own conclusion. Viv stood up, reached into her pocket, and pulled out a crumbly piece of scone.

'I didn't do anything wrong.' Viv stuffed the scone into her mouth. Pania knew she imagined marrying Brett one day, had already picked out the dress. It was long in the back, shorter at the front.

'You new girls are all the same,' Simone said. 'But you're as complicit as anyone, Viv. Guarantee you've paid his bail more than once. And probably his rent as well.'

Viv's cheeks flushed as she chewed, then swallowed. Brett always accused Viv of not being loyal, when Pania knew for a fact he slept with a lot of women. They were always arguing about something. 'I wasn't fucking born yesterday,' he said. The drugs made him paranoid and Viv loved the drugs as well as Brett and it was a shit slide. There was an expectation Viv was on hold, on call.

'You'd be stupid not to be on your own side,' Simone said.

Viv kept talking in a low voice telling Pania they could leave together, get an office job in Ohakune. Pania couldn't blame Viv. It was Brett she hated, for ruining everything.

'Viv, I'm sorry. But I can't leave.' Viv had never been any good at negotiations. She felt she owed the world. That was the heart of it.

Pania wanted to know what the Vandenbergs wanted, exactly.

'Apart from all the land,' Simone laughed. 'And paying us what they think we're worth. They make us think we're lucky to be here.'

It was a shock to Pania when Brett got out of the taxi, looking like a different person, although that part was predictable. He was probably trying to avoid going back to jail. He'd cut his hair short, and it was a different colour. Some things were the same, the smile and those eyes with the rings that needed sleep. His bag clinked with the sound of bottles as he put it on the ground. He kissed Viv and gave her a bunch of expensive looking flowers and wouldn't meet Pania's eyes. They sat on the ground in front of their A-frame. The shadows from the A-frames made a star-like formation of dark and light on the ground. Faces peered down at them from surrounding windows. Viv was talking about something, about how she'd wished Brett here. She wasn't making much sense. Around Brett, Viv became the opposite of who she was. She couldn't say no to Brett either. And Brett, he just liked people to do things for him.

He pulled a bottle out of his bag and opened it. It had no label on it. He handed it to Viv.

'Cheers,' Viv said, holding the bottle up, and Brett said cheers and Pania didn't.

She wanted to say, 'Why are you here now, why have you come?'

'Celebrating. Like old times,' and Viv drank from the bottle. Men like Brett could smell shame and he got off on humiliating women, but specifically Viv.

He took something else out of his bag and held it up. 'New phone, babe. It's all set up, ready to go.'

Viv chewed on a thumbnail, not looking at Pania.

'I promise I'm never gonna let you go again,' he said. 'I'm gonna find us a house.'

'I've got to get to work.' Viv ran inside, laughing like a child. They'd never lived together, not officially.

Pania looked out over the lawn. A patch of grass between the A-frames and the track had been bleached brown in the sun. The top of her head felt hot.

'Relax, sweetheart,' Brett said. 'I'm glad we understand each other. You look beautiful when you're moody, by the way.'

She was ready for him. For too long she'd been convinced that nobody would understand how she got into this situation. 'There's no understanding here, Brett.'

'That's where you're wrong, Pania. I think there's a mutual need. It just takes a bit of honesty,' Brett said, taking a sip from the bottle. 'Viv said you'd be sensitive about things.'

'There's no need, Brett.' But she meant for him to be there. 'And fuck off with your honesty.' She lowered her voice. 'We left that woman to die, Brett.'

He laughed. 'That's your version of events. You must have been totally gone, Pania. You might want to lay off things for a while, you're sounding like a deranged bitch.'

'I'm not the one who needs to lay off anything. How about you lay off Viv?'

'What's with the tone, love?' he said. 'Bit jealous of me and Viv's fresh start?'

The last thing Pania wanted was to be friends. She wanted to shout that he made her leave the woman there.

The A-frame was different with him there. Viv wasn't just happier, she was hooked. While they worked, he slept, only coming outside for cigarettes. Things seemed good at first, and even the A-frame women thought he was gorgeous. But it wasn't long before the arguments started again. Viv was on edge again. There were days when they didn't see him, then days when they did.

One night, when Viv was late back from a busy night shift, Brett threw her belongings out the window into the A-frame circle. Simone went out and picked everything up, and shortly after, Brett showed up at her door threatening to break things – the door, the bed.

'Better for him not to be here. Better for everyone,' Helena said. You have to take responsibility for this, Viv. It needs to be you for it to work.'

Pania wanted to say something to Viv, to try and comfort her but Viv was calm, fastidiously tucking in the sheet corners. Nobody had thought of this until now, that Brett might not accept anyone else. Pania saw it dawning on her, with the knowledge that it had to happen soon. She looked out the window. There was a dark shape moving up the track towards the car park. If Brett left now someone would give him a lift, to Taupō or anywhere he could get a motel. Surely there was another way?

'All right,' Viv said, her voice low and resigned. It was as though she'd accepted the truth from Helena, scared of her proposal but able to be persuaded.

Pania heard herself making stupid jokes, talking about the weather, unable to say what she meant: let's go.

That night Pania saw Viv's laughing face and knew she'd begun to feel differently about Brett.

'We don't need him,' Viv said. 'I'll do it.'

'We'll be right behind you,' said Pania. Maybe there wasn't another way.

'I'll need some things.'

'Anything you need.'

It took some doing but Viv finally managed to get Brett out of bed, out of the A-frame.

'It's our anniversary,' she lied, as it wasn't that sort of relationship. Viv saw that now. She needed some protection against it all, against Brett, against the woman he'd left to die.

'Remember how we met?' She knew he was itching to be gone, already imagining himself on the motorway to Auckland.

'At the club.' It was a safe guess.

From across the club, Brett's smile had screamed *boys will be boys* to Viv. Everyone stood too close and engaged in unnecessary touch and women who were barely more than girls rushed at Brett, kissing him on both cheeks. He'd possibly fucked them at some point, it was impossible to know. But she couldn't help it. He slid an arm around Viv's waist and told her to stick her tongue out. The pill he had made her love him terribly and love the girl-women and buy drinks for them all. The pills altered everything.

Later, less ready to comply, Viv tried to lay down some rules for the relationship, but he smiled and ignored her. If she flirted with someone else, she got a warning, but he could fuck who he liked. She couldn't give him up, but she couldn't afford to get secure.

They set off through the trees, with a picnic, towards the river. It felt like it could rain.

'We've missed the best of the day.' It was no good rushing him when everything necessary was on hand. No one had put it all together yet, but they would.

'Why did you come?' she finally asked him, but he didn't answer, only shrugged.

He brought out a jar of pills and unscrewed the top.

Viv held out her palm and he shook one onto it. They couldn't be more than five minutes away.

'Are they strong?'

'Yeah, but the comedowns are sweet.' He thought he'd got away with it.

She deliberated, like it made all the difference in the world. 'What was her name? The girl Pania found?'

She scanned his face for any emotion. The truth of what happened, and what he did. This was part of their practice. The hard part came when people forgot what happened to them. 'You can tell me her first name, or anything you know about her, when you're ready.'

'Babe. Can we just shut up about the dead girl?' Soon, he would wish he had a choice in the matter.

'I mean, given her age, and where she lived, it must have been easy to track her details down, online.'

'Babe. What about this picnic?'

Viv pulled an orange out of her pocket and started peeling it. She could stop fighting now. The trees rearranged their shadows and she glanced towards them, knowing the women were waiting.

Acknowledgements

I am very grateful to Creative New Zealand and the Louis Johnson New Writer's Bursary – the funding made finishing this book possible.

To the Michael King Centre, and the Robert Lord Cottage, for the space to write.

To Pip Adam, thank you for your generous mentorship and asking the hard questions of the work. This book is better because of you.

To Maiangi Waitai, for the incredible cover artwork which supports this book.

Thank you to Emily Perkins, my MA supervisor, and classmates – in particular Rachel Kerr, Linley Boniface and Raqi Syed for your friendship, for reading many drafts and your intelligent, honest feedback.

To William Brandt. Those deadlines and writing meetings kept me writing in the two years after I became a parent. You gave so generously of your time.

To Aidan Rasmussen and Pip Adam, your insights and friendship helped get me over the line.

To Te Hā o Ngā Pou Taranaki Kaituhi Māori for tautoko and kōrero. To Steph Matuku, for the facetimes and the memes.

To James George, for a valuable manuscript assessment of an early draft. Tēnā rawa atu koe.

To the NZSA for the opportunity to apply for mentorships and manuscript assessment.

To essa may ranapiri for providing final hour feedback.

To Mauraka Edwards. Kā mihi mo tō whānaukataka mai.

Kelly McCosh, for the key to your peaceful home, even when I haven't made it there.

Thank you to Te Herenga Waka University Press – Anna Knox, for your impeccable editorial guidance. Your questions and nudges made this book much better. Fergus Barrowman, Ashleigh Young, Craig Gamble, Tayi Tibble and Kirsten McDougall. This book is better because of all of you. Thanks also to Ebony Lamb for the author photo.

To Lenni for being the best possible distraction and for the best conversations. To Muzz, this book was a long time in the making and wouldn't have been possible without your love and support.

To my friends, all of whom I love dearly and a few of whom read early drafts of these stories.

To my family. Thank you for everything.

Versions of some of the stories in this collection first appeared elsewhere. 'Ruin' in the Verb Festival 2021 publication; 'The Game' in *Sport* (Issue 47, 2019) and Newsroom in 2019; 'Housewarming' in *Ika* (Issue 4, 2016); 'Scarce Objects' (as 'Mangrove Heights') in *Huia 14*; 'Missing' in *Takahē* (December, 2022); 'Fur' in *Hue and Cry* (Issue 8); 'Previous Selves' in *Hugh Morrieson Literary Journal*, 2021; 'Shadow' in *Sport* (Issue 44, 2016); 'Sweet on the Comedown' in *Sport* (Issue 42, 2014); 'Doctor Ink' (as 'Biding her Time') in *Action, Spectacle* (February, 2021). Thank you to the editors and publishers for your support.